"A taut, fraught look at tragedy, its aftermath, and the stories we tell ourselves to survive. With suspense, dread, and always the possibility for redemption, we watch as Zambrano flips the cards of chance and fate."

—Justin Torres, author of *We the Animals*

"This novel seems simple and straightforward at first; in fact, *Lotería* is anything but that: Mario Alberto Zambrano's wonderful book is constructed as a beautiful, gripping, and lyrical set of riddles (asked and solved) about life-and-death matters in one family. Like the novels of Cortázar, its form is intricate and beautiful."

—Charles Baxter, author of *Gryphon: New and Selected Stories* and *The Feast of Love*

"In *Lotería*, Zambrano performs a lyrical and formal sleight of hand, conjuring a spiritually profound and deeply moving story of one young girl's struggle to reconcile her losses and leave nothing to chance. . . . This gorgeous, one-of-a-kind debut marks the emergence of a singular and powerful new literary voice."

—Amber Dermont, *New York Times* bestselling author of *The Starboard Sea* and *Damage Control: Stories*

"In a bold, deeply felt debut, Zambrano brings us tragedy made powerful. . . . These are people who hold on to each other so hard it hurts. And this moving novel will hug you too, every bit as tight."

—Josh Weil, author of *The New Valley*

"Sometimes what Zambrano leaves off the page is just as important as what's been written. This narrative sleight of hand shows Zambrano's gift for evoking great pain in stark, lyrical sketches."   —*Los Angeles Times*

"*Lotería* should delight and disturb any reader sensitive to the ways of children and how they think and, more importantly, how deeply they feel."

—*Dallas Morning News*

"Zambrano uses his string of short-story-like entries effectively to make Luz a many-faceted diamond, hardened by life but still filled with light and beauty."

—*Minneapolis Star Tribune*

"*Lotería* . . . captures, from a wide-eyed yet uncloying child's perspective, the ways in which life can feel a lot like a game of chance."   —*Vogue,* "Summer Reads"

"[Zambrano's] debut novel . . . is a polished tome of prose unreeling the tale of plucky little Luz María Castillo in the game of chance called life. . . . We peer like voyeurs, artfully led by Zambrano's pacing, dialogue, and comically drawn characters."   —*Houston Chronicle*

"Zambrano's stellar debut is proof positive that good things come in small packages. Here the good thing—dare we say, the very good thing?—is the journal/memoir of eleven-year-old Luz Castillo, who has been taken into the state's custody after her father is arrested. . . . Although this spare, little illustrated book may seem better suited to young adult readers, rest assured that Luz's story will engage both young and old right up to, and beyond, the startling plot twist."

—*Booklist* (starred review)

"An incredible first novel."   —*Village Voice*

"His restraint from sentimentality, his mastery of well-made sentences, and his rich imagination lift words off the page— like dancers in a ballet."   —*National Post* (Canada)

"The broken tale and imaginative first-person narration lend weight to this curious novel. It's an impressive first step for an artist exploring a new medium."

—*Kirkus Reviews*

"This is a smart and powerful tale, beautifully rendered by a sensitive artist."   —*Shelf Awareness*

"*Lotería* reaches a rare plane where it transcends its form and comes alive as a commentary on character, family, and culture."   —*Brooklyn Rail*

"This is a gripping, heartbreaking novel by a new writer who already understands the power of understatement and controlled revelation."   —*El Paso Times*

"Luz's (and by extension Zambrano's) refusal to give in to easy condemnations of her father's actions, beautifully highlighted by genuinely difficult arguments between Luz and Estrella, is among this novel's most risky and ultimately successful gambits."

—*School Library Journal* (starred review)

LOTERÍA

* * * * * * * * *

A Novel

Mario Alberto Zambrano

HARPER PERENNIAL

NEW YORK • LONDON • TORONTO • SYDNEY • NEW DELHI • AUCKLAND

A hardcover edition of this book was published in 2013 by Harper-Collins Publishers.

P.S.™ is a trademark of HarperCollins Publishers.

HarperCollins books may be purchased for educational, business, or sales promotional use. For information please e-mail the Special Markets Department at SPsales@harpercollins.com.

FIRST HARPER PERENNIAL EDITION PUBLISHED 2014.

All illustrations by Jarrod Taylor

Library of Congress Cataloging-in-Publication Data has been applied for.

ISBN 978-0-06-226855-6 (pbk.)

20 21 22 23   OV/LSC   10 9 8 7 6 5 4 3 2

for my mother,
for my father

RULES *of the* GAME

*L*otería is often described as Mexican bingo, a game of chance. The only material difference between bingo and *Lotería* is that bingo relies on a grid of numbers while *Lotería* relies on images.

There are fifty-four cards and each comes with a riddle, *un dicho*. There is a traditional set of riddles, but sometimes dealers create their own to trick the players. After the dealer "sings" the riddle the players cover the appropriate spots on their playing boards, their *tablas*, with either bottle caps, dried beans, or loose change.

There is more than one way to win depending on what is played. You can win by filling a vertical line, a horizontal line, a diagonal; the four corners, the center squares, or a blackout.

An important rule to remember is that a winner must shout his victory as soon as his winning image is called. If the dealer calls another riddle before the winner declares *¡Lotería!*, the player can no longer claim his prize.

El que es buen gallo,
en cualquier gallinero canta.

LOTERÍA

* * * * * *

33

LA ARAÑA

LA ARAÑA

This room has spiders.

¿*Y?* It's not like You don't see them. The way they move their legs and carry their backs and creep in the dark when you're not looking. You see us, ¿*verdad?* You see what we see? It's not like You don't know what we're thinking when we lie down at night and look up at the ceiling, or when we crawl in our heads the way these spiders crawl over furniture. It's never made sense why people think You're only there at church and nowhere else. Not at home or in the yard or the police station. Or under a bed.

When I first walked in there was a wooden desk and a chair that wobbled when I sat in it, next to a thin bed with a green blanket. Tencha said the room needed something so she started buying me roses from the flower shop in Magnolia Park and putting them on the windowsill. From one day to the next I watch the petals fall to the floor and that's when I notice the spiders. They crawl to the cracks in the wall when she comes to visit then crawl out again when she leaves. I'm at my desk doing what she told me to do, because she said I should write as much as I can, even if it's one word, one sentence. Let the cards help you, mama. *Échale ganas.*

My name is Luz. Luz María Castillo. And I'm eleven years old. You've known me since before I was born, I'm sure, but I want to start from the beginning. Because who else should I speak to but You?

It's been five days since I've been here and I don't have anything but a week's worth of clothes and a deck of *Lotería*. The best thing to do now is to be patient and co-operative, they say, otherwise I'll be sent to *Casa de Esperanza*. Tencha can't have custody, not unless we move back to Mexico, and they say that whenever I'm ready to talk it'll make things easier. But Tencha told them she filed her papers and has been working here for eight years, so why don't they let me go? Why can't she take me? I'm waiting for the day she walks in and tells me to pack my bags because we're going home, wherever that is.

Julia's a counselor here and looks like she could be in college, skinny and black, but gringa-looking by the things she wears. She tries to talk to me at lunch as she flips her hair to one side like a feathered wing. She brings me issues of *Fama* magazine and points to the photos and asks, "Like her music? She's pretty, huh?"

Then she looks at me like if I'm one of those stories you hear about on the ten o'clock news. Like one of those women who leave their kids in the car with the windows rolled up while they go grocery shopping. Or a story about some punk kid who molests a girl after school. Or some father who finds out his son's gay and rams a broomstick up his butt until it bleeds. And whoever reports the story on the news channel has this concerned look over her face standing outside the hospital room where the son's recovering. She

— 3 —

looks into the camera and repeats what the father said to his son as he stood over him with the broomstick in his hand: "You sure you want to be gay, son?"

I'm Papi's daughter, but still. That story is a true story and that boy was my age and when I saw him on television, I felt bad for him. I wanted to spit in that newscaster's face, the way she pretended like she cared. To her it was just another story, but to that boy, he must've been sore, must've been hurting real bad and wondering what it was going to be like once he got home.

There's a guy named Ricardo staying in one of the rooms on the opposite side of the building. He has dreadlocks that fall to his knees but he twists them the way you wring a mop and plops them on his head. One night we were watching *The Price Is Right* in the common room and he told me he liked to do something called blow. His foster parents found him cutting lines on the kitchen counter and that's why they turned him in. That's why he's getting counseling. He said *Casa de Esperanza* is where they take kids when nobody wants them. After Tencha saw him she told me to stay away from him.

— 4 —

When I'm sitting by myself by the window doodling on paper, Julia comes up to me and tries to act like she's my best friend. "What are you drawing?" she asks. "I can help you. Why don't you let me help you?" Then she sits there, staring at me.

¿Y? It's not like I'm a piece of news in the *Chronicle* she can pick up and read. It's not like that. If anything, it's a *telenovela* with a *ranchera* in the background playing so loud you can't even hear your thoughts anymore. Like that movie *Nosotros los pobres*, when Pedro Infante is accused of killing his wife. He didn't do it and only his daughter Chachita believes him. Half the movie is not knowing what happened, whether he killed her or not. Everyone thinks he's guilty, but he's not. He's just poor. Chachita visits him in jail and pleads to the officers to let him go. She has braids in pigtails and throws her arms over her head like Hallelujah! She falls to the floor, crying with tears over her cheeks, all slobbery, all dramatic, like one of those old ladies at church who's lost her husband, praying, *¿Por qué me haces esto, Señor? ¡Por favor, Dios mio!*

Tencha says I should tell Julia whatever she wants to know. If I don't want to talk then I should write it down because we have to get Papi out of jail. That way we can go home and be together again. The only way he can get out of jail is if I open up, she says.

"Why don't you use the cards to help you, mama? *Andale*. Write it down in a journal, like that they can see what happened. Like that they can see he didn't do anything wrong."

At first, I didn't want to. I didn't feel like it. Besides, Tencha wouldn't believe me. Or maybe she would. Maybe she knows what it was like but never wanted to believe it in the first place because she loves her brother too much. Either way, I'm keeping this as mine.

What I write is for You and me and no one else.

There's this spider at the edge of my desk and she's looking at me like if I'm her *Virgen de Guadalupe*. I don't want her touching me or getting too close, and I know she's not poisonous, but still. I could blow her off in one breath if I wanted to. I'm thinking of smashing her, then cleaning her off with my sock and acting like it never happened. But when I raise my hand and close my eyes I hear her scream.

Julia says the reason I don't say anything is because I'm in deep pain. Like if pain were something she knew looked like me. I hear her when she talks to Tencha outside my room. Because I'm eleven she treats me like some kid. The way she looks at me, feeling sorry for me, scared, but at the same time frustrated. Like if answers are overdue and behind her pity she's upset that I'm not "cooperating."

I used to tell You I pray for Your will. *¿Recuerdas?* I used to make the sign of the cross in the dark while I was in bed and tell you how much I loved You. That I wish for the best and I pray for your will. Well, I do, but maybe I'll smash this spider. Mom used to say that life was full of tests. And if we pass, we'll be in Your grace. Maybe if she named me *Milagro* instead of *Luz* this would've never happened.

If I wait for this spider to crawl out of this room, then maybe I can go after her. And on the other side of this wall there'll be this underwater world and I'll swim to the deep end and float next to one of those electrical fish that light up in the dark. And maybe he'll sting me or split me into pieces or eat me alive. But then everything will be over and no one will remember because I'll be down there in the dark with nothing around me. With no fish, no light. No Luz.

Then what?

48

LA CHALUPA

LA CHALUPA

There's a flea market on Alexander Street that we used to go to when I was little. It's where we went to buy things like *comales* and *molcajetes*. They sold sheets and sheets of *Lotería* paper and I didn't know it came rolled up like that. I didn't know you could make your own *tabla*.

There was a round woman who sat in a canoe with flowerpots around her like if they were her children. Red flowers, pink, yellow, and purple. She wore a nightgown with thin stripes and had braids falling down her chest. Her name was Alondra. Estrella called her *una pendeja* because she was a grown woman dressed up like a *Lotería* card. But she wasn't dumb. She made bracelets with all these different colors and would stitch your name on one if you asked. Two dollars apiece. She'd sit under the sun, even when it was ninety-five degrees outside, and braid her bracelets. We'd pass her on the way to the food stands, buy some *barbacoa* and *tamarindo*, then pass her again, and she'd be in the same place.

"Want something, Alondra? *¿Un Jarrito? ¿Algo? Ándale*," Papi would say.

She'd close her eyes and tighten them, shake her head like if she were remembering someone who'd died. When she'd open her eyes we'd notice she wasn't crying. *"No, no gracias,"* she'd say. *"No necesito nada."* She'd open her arms and sweat would be glistening over her forehead.

I asked her to write a word on each bracelet I bought because I wanted them to read like a sentence. *Ven. Que. Te. Quiero. Ahora.* It's the riddle to *La Rosa*, which is a strange *dicho*. I don't know how a rose has anything to do with wanting or loving. But every time I thought of it I heard Mom's voice and the way she'd say it in Spanish, all smooth and sexy like Sara Montiel: Come, I want you now.

And because *quiero* can mean either want or love, I asked if it meant "I want you" or "I love you." Come here, because I *love* you, or, come here, because I *want* you? If you were saying to someone, *come* to me, then the person you loved wasn't there, and if you had to tell someone to *come* to you then maybe he didn't love you. And to *want* someone to come to you is like an order. If you have to order someone to *come* to you, how much love is in that anyway?

After Alondra made my last bracelet, I put it on my arm and she read them out loud from my wrist to my elbow. *Ven. Que. Te. Quiero. Ahora.* She opened her arms and hugged me the way Tencha does, with her body soft like pillows, and I understood why even though she was smiling sometimes she looked like she was in pain. She was confused of whether or not she was wanting or loving. Or both.

44

EL CANTARITO

EL CANTARITO

When Estrella ran away I thought she was going to Angélica's house because she wanted to scare Papi into thinking she was leaving for good. We thought she was being dramatic and wanting attention. I never thought she'd go to the cops. I never thought they'd come to the house the way they did.

Julia asks the same thing over and over when she sits down next to me in the activity room. She wants to know what it was like living at home. "And on weekends?" she asks. "What did you do all together? What did you do with your Papi?" But she wouldn't get it. She wouldn't know what it was like.

We all fought. We all hit each other.

Papi punched because he was a man, but we hit him too. There was one time when Mom grabbed the Don Pedro bottle from the coffee table and smashed it over his head. Blood ran down his face like the statue of Jesus Christ and Estrella and I had to grab toilet paper to soak up the blood.

Now, here comes Julia thinking *Fama* magazine is going to open me up like some stupid jack-in-the-box. Like if I'm some extension cord tangled up in a garage she can take a few minutes to untangle. Then what? She'll leave me alone? Or maybe Papi will stay in jail because of something I say, something she writes down and tangles up later.

It's like in *Lotería*, instead of playing the four corners we play the center squares. But midway through the game you find you have the corners but you're missing the center. And if you would've played the corners you would've won already. But that's how it is, isn't it?

I keep my mouth shut because I don't know the rules of the game.

Three days ago Tencha came to visit me and sat in the chair next to the door. I'd been laying out the cards on my desk. *La Rana*. *El Paraguas*. *El Melón*. Thinking about the stories the cards helped me remember. Usually she sits with me on the bed and rocks me back and forth and tells me everything's going to be okay. But this time she sat in the chair, all hunched over with her feet together, and whispered, "Mama." Then nothing. Like if she couldn't get the rest of the sentence out. I knew what she was trying to tell me, that her rosaries for the last week were for nothing. Her prayers to *la Virgen* were for nothing. And if I waited for her to tell me it would've taken too long. So I walked over to her and put my hand on her shoulder, and she started sobbing in that way that's scary, like if her lungs are falling out and she has to suck them back in before they fall to the floor.

Estrella was in the ICU ever since that night they came to get Papi. I was looking out the window next to my desk when Tencha asked if I wanted to see her. She whispered, like if I'd get mad at her for mentioning her name. But she knew it wasn't going to be the way I imagined. I wouldn't sit at the end of Estrella's bed and hold her hand. And I wouldn't be able to go inside the room she was in. When Tencha said her name I put on my sneakers and stood up, keeping my head down so I wouldn't have to see her eyes.

She had to get permission, she said. Larry, the social services director, didn't think it was a good idea. He lowered his voice as he talked to her in the hall, but I could hear him. He said I was too fragile, it might make me worse. But she told him good, said if I didn't get to see my sister I'd sue him when I turned eighteen. My own flesh and blood. They should be ashamed of themselves. "Shame on you!" she said. And then he agreed, but only for one night. She told him everything would be fine. She was responsible and this was a family matter.

Before we walked out of the building he told us an officer would take us to the hospital and sign us in. We drove to the Medical Center near the zoo off of highway 59, to a huge building that looked like a good place, not some clinic with bums crowding the emergency room. It looked like a place that could fix things. It had forty-four floors and there were doctors with clipboards walking up and down the hallway. When we asked the receptionist for Estrella María Castillo the woman told us she was on the thirty-eighth floor. I remember because I pushed the button in the elevator but it wouldn't light up, and when the doors opened the hallway was quiet. It seemed like no one was there. But finally a nurse passed. She said I couldn't go inside the room where Estrella was. All I could do was see her from behind a pane of glass. But all I could see was her chin and the shape of her body past two other beds. I couldn't see her eyes. There was a curtain blocking half of her face. For all I knew it could've been someone else.

When the nurse looked at me she did that tilt of the head like people do, like if I were abandoned. Other nurses started to show up and they looked at me in the same way. Maybe they thought I'd attack them or knock them over or run inside the room no matter what I was told, because they'd heard what had happened. But I didn't. I stood there and looked at my sister while Tencha walked with them down the hall and asked them questions.

The machines that were next to her beeped louder the longer I stayed, and no matter how much I tried to block them out, I couldn't. I pressed my palms against the glass and told her how much I love her. How sorry I was. My sister. Just there, sleeping. Not moving. She got blurry from the fog of my breath covering the glass, and I whispered, *¿Y por qué tenías que ser tan tonta?* I wrote her name in my mind and imagined the star as I drew it over the glass.

Mom used to say to us, *Estrella y Luz, cuánto las quiero.*

I pressed my hands harder against the glass and told her it was going to be okay, not because You were going to make it okay but because I was there and You were there and I was really trying to tell You something. Like how much I love You. And if I loved You, wouldn't that make things better? It didn't matter if I fell on my knees or threw up my hands and prayed I don't know how many Hail Marys. *Lo siento, Madre María.* But it was a matter of Your will. Learn to live with what you lose and that's what's meant to be. *¿Verdad?* Mom used to say, "Forgive and forget." I say it to myself over and over when I'm trying to fall asleep at night but it feels like a lie. It turns into a song and then I don't even know what I'm singing anymore.

Standing there, all of a sudden, I was like a jug of water trying to be taken from one place to another, and little by little, I was spilling. The nurses didn't even look at me anymore.

EL VALIENTE

EL VALIENTE

Pancho Silva was fat and never showered. He had gray hair on the sides of his head and a little on top that he combed forward. He told Papi when he first met him that he was going to be a movie star. He was in that Pedro Infante movie *Los tres huastecos* as a double and was working his way up. He and Pedro Infante were tight, like brothers. But after Pedro's death in a plane crash Pancho's future as a film star was over. He told Papi the job at the industrial plant was just temporary, and he was planning on getting back into the movies someday. *Puro* bullshit

Papi said. And it's true. When I met Pancho Silva he didn't look a thing like Pedro Infante. He *is* full of shit, I said, and Papi agreed because he winked at me.

Papi met him at the bakery down the block from our house on TC Jester one morning when some black guy walked in with spandex on his head. Pancho was standing in front of Papi, and he turned around and said something under his breath about the spandex. Papi smiled, because he's polite. Then Pancho started talking to him in Spanish, asking him where he was from, if he had a job. He said he could get him something at the plant he worked at because he was retiring soon and they'd need someone to replace him.

That day, Papi brought home *tres leches*. Mom said it was too sweet and runny and it didn't have enough eggs. She said the one her Tía Sofi makes is the best in the world and no other *tres leches* comes close. You could only have a slice of this one with a cup of coffee or a glass of water to wash it down. Estrella didn't say anything, but I could tell she liked hers because she kept licking her fork. But none of that mattered. Papi smiled and said to us, *"Ya tengo trabajo."*

After his first day at work he said the plant stunk. It was hard to breathe because of the lack of air. He had to punch in at five-thirty in the morning and work until six in the evening, carrying sheets of metal and putting them where they belonged. Then push a button. Sometimes they'd ask him to help in other departments, like welding. They'd show him what to do, and he'd do it. *Como un pinche perro*, he'd say. He came home with his arms covered in black. Sweaty. Tired. Worn-out. And that's when I'd get him a beer from the kitchen. I'd cut a lime and squeeze juice over it, because beer is better that way. Then I'd take a sip to make sure it tasted good. Like that, I'd get a little *peda también*. One beer turned into two, then three, then a six-pack. Then I started seeing a glass half-filled with Don Pedro by the couch. Sometimes at night I'd be going to sleep and hear him singing *rancheras* in the backyard. If I was still awake, I'd go out there and sing. I'd tell Estrella to come with me, but she'd roll her eyes and say she wasn't a drunk Mexican like Papi.

"Mija linda," he'd sing, his arms reaching toward the sky and his hips swaying. He'd hum some *ranchera*

and I'd try to figure out which one it was. Mom would open the back door wearing nothing but an oversized T-shirt and tell us to be quiet before she even asked what we were doing. Papi would hit his chest with both fists, like Tarzan, like if that would make him louder, and say, *"¡Aaaaaaaaaayyyyyyy, pero qué chorrito de voz tengo!"* I'd laugh, and she would too. We'd laugh so hard it'd take me awhile before I could sing. Then finally, we'd sing. The same song, always, all together, all three of us.

"Paloma negra, paloma negra."

Until I fell asleep and Papi would carry me to bed.

13

EL GORRITO

EL GORRITO

When we'd get ready for church it was like if *misa* were in some rich person's house. Mom would spit in her hand and flatten my hair, wipe my face and say, *"¡Arréglate ya, niña!"*

In our room, Estrella would stand in front of our full-length mirror trying to decide what to wear. She taped photographs from teen magazines all over our walls with the singers from Menudo, Rob Lowe, and Scott Baio. It was like they were watching her as she got ready. She'd hold a curling iron above her head and count to twelve.

"Why you curling your hair?" I'd ask. "They're just going to fall when you go outside." She'd ignore me and mumble something about the color of her eyes and how she wished they were green, like Mom's. She'd spray Aqua Net like if it were Lysol and put a barrette in her hair. Usually a bow made of ribbon. Sometimes a plastic flower.

All I did was make sure my hair was out of my face.

In Mom's bathroom I'd sit on the toilet and watch her take out her rollers. She'd paint her eyes with different shades of orange and cover her lips with a tint of red, spray perfume on her neck and under her wrists, then walk into her closet and slip on a dress with the back zipper left open. With her high heels hooked on her finger and her earrings in place and her necklace sitting above her collarbone, she'd turn around and ask, "How do I look?"

"You're beautiful," I'd say, and she'd walk out the bedroom door.

I remember the smell of Papi's cologne as he walked down the hallway, the sound of his black leather boots against the wooden floor. Gray pants. Button-up shirt. I wanted to be the mini version of him. Dressed like twins. But I had to wear a dress.

• • •

After Papi and Mom moved to America we didn't have our family anymore. I remember Abuela Topazio, Mom's mom, but only a little. She died when we were young. Mom used to show me pictures of her holding me when I was a baby, when she lived in Reynosa before we moved here. Sometimes I'd act like I remembered things to make her feel better. "She used to make us *caldo*, right? With bits of ground beef? We'd put ketchup and lime juice in it to cover up the taste of animal fat."

Abuelo died too, when Mom was a teenager. He was coming home from work on the bus and some dog stepped out in the middle of the road while the driver was telling someone to sit down. He swerved into a ditch and the bus tipped over.

Mom was the only girl, the only child, no brother, no sister. Her *tíos* lived too far south to ever see them.

Tencha is my *tía*, Papi's older sister by two years, and

we call her Tencha because it's easier than Hortencia. When we're together she says to me, "We're tight, mama. *Somos iguales*." She came with Mom and Papi when they left Reynosa, and my Tío Carlos, Papi's younger brother, stayed in Mexico with his two sons, Memo and Félix, *mis primos*. We never met Papi's mom, Abuela Luz, who I'm named after, because she died too.

Now that I write it down it seems everyone died, and maybe they're next to You sitting around a table playing games. The only one left is Buelo Fermín, Papi's dad. He doesn't do much but sit in his rocking chair and cough loud. We used to visit him in Reynosa during summer vacation, sometimes Christmas, but all we did was listen to him tell stories about when he was a boy. How he'd spin a rooster by its head only to snap it off and watch it dance until it died.

After coming to Magnolia Park we met our second family after Papi met Pancho. And it was with them we played *Lotería* every Sunday after church. Maybe that's why they felt like family. There was Buelita Fe, Pancho's wife. Then Tía Elsa and Tío Fernando, Tío Jesús and

Tía Hilda. They weren't our real aunts and uncles but we called them *tíos* because it was easier. Then there was Gastón and Miriam, the youngest like me, then Luisa, four years older than Estrella.

At home, before leaving to see them, we'd be dressed and smelling good and walk to the car to head over to Pancho's house. I'd walk slowly so I could see them in front of me, Papi, Mom, and Estrella. And when it was sunny, so sunny I had to squint, Mom would wear her movie-star hat with a blue ribbon around it. She'd see me walking behind them, all slow, then snap her fingers. "Luz! Get your butt over here and put your shoes on."

And I would. I'd crawl into the backseat and put on my shoes and we'd be off to go see the Silvas.

24

EL COTORRO

EL COTORRO

You heard about Memo? He blew up his hand with a firecracker. They said his fingers flew off in pieces and it looked like his hand had been eaten by a dog. Tío Carlos called and told Papi, and Papi told me afterward. He said they were at the hospital. "Why didn't he let go?" I asked. "Your Tío Carlos said it just got stuck in his hand." "How stuck? What do you mean, stuck?" It didn't make sense. When we'd go to Reynosa Memo and his friends would always light *cuetes*. But their firecrackers aren't like the ones here. *Cuetes* in Mexico are made of cement and look like pieces of thick chalk. "One of those gray ones?" "Yes, Luz, one of those gray ones." "Really? I can't imagine how much that hurt." "Well, go pray for your cousin."

Maybe this was Your way of punishing him. For that time when I lost a bet in marbles and was pissed because I was good at *canicas*, but every time I threw the ball Memo would push me off balance and he'd win. Then he told me to go with him to the back of the store, where they put the chickens. He was older than me, already a man, Tío Carlos said. He wasn't mean, always included me in games and asked me if I wanted to go somewhere, to some *mercado* or to the *Plaza de San Pedro* to throw rocks at pigeons.

It was just the two of us. Everyone else went to *el rancho* with a friend of my Tío's and Estrella was with Mom. Papi was somewhere, I don't remember. Memo took me to the place between the fence and the coop and he grabbed my hand and put it between his legs, like if he was sharing a secret. And what I felt was a baby's arm. I remember it throbbing in the way a *gallina's* wings tremble when you hold it between your hands. "What do you want me to do?" I said.

"Masajéalo," he said. *"Despacito."*

His thing got bigger and harder and he licked his lips. Then we heard the back door of a house slam and he pushed me away and ran back to the house.

● ● ●

The night I found out he blew up his hand, I waited for all the lights to turn off in the house.

"Estrella?" I said.

She was sleeping. I snuck up next to her bed and kneeled on the floor, pushed her shoulder. "Estrella? Wake up." "What?" "Guess what?" "What?" She made that face like if she were looking at the ugliest thing in the world.

"Memo blew up his hand *con un cuete* and now he has just one finger left. The rest of them blew off."

"So?"

And that was it.

3

LA DAMA

LA DAMA

Sometimes I like to write in the morning after I wake up because in a way I feel like I'm dreaming. No one else is awake and my thoughts are the only thing I can hear. There's a cleaning lady who comes to mop the hallway, and the way I know she's there is because of the smell of Pine-Sol coming in from under the door. It reminds me of Mom and the way she liked to clean.

And today, look who I turn over from the top of the deck, *La Dama*.

• • •

Every Sunday, without fail, Pancho Silva and Buelita Fe expected us over at their house. We'd arrive and she'd be boiling water for *fideos* and he'd be wearing his cowboy hat, slumped in his armchair watching *luchadores* on a black-and-white television. Their house was a block away from the interstate, but with all the branches surrounding the screened-in porch it felt like a tree house.

The first thing I'd do when we got there is run inside and sneak into the shoebox under the cabinet where she kept *Lotería tablas*. I'd find mine at the bottom without even looking, just feeling with my hand like some blind person searching for a coin. She had sheets of *Lotería* rolled up like wrapping paper from when she'd go visit her sisters in Mexico. I used to cut the images out and make my own *tablas*. I'd arrange them the way I liked so that I didn't have to choose a board that came already packaged. One time I wanted to cut out sixteen images of *La Sirena* and make a *tabla* filled with sixteen mermaids. Like that, I'd win whenever she was called. But I figured it'd be boring to play that way, so instead I cut out images of *La Araña* and glued them to the corners.

We used Sharpies to write our names on the back of our boards. Miriam covered the back of hers with bubble letters and Luisa drew flowers over the "I" in hers. Gastón wrote "Property of Gastón Silva" in the corner with such neat handwriting you could tell he was trying to make it perfect. Some *tablas* weren't even glued on cardboard to keep them stiff. They were just sheets of paper and they curled like pencil shavings. Some had people's names on the back I didn't recognize. Like Marcella. Who was she? Luisa would sometimes take her *tabla* during a game and bet three quarters on it, to try her luck. And she'd win! I remember Marcella's name because her *tabla* was always the lucky one. Whoever played it would win at least three or four times.

• • •

Once everyone arrived at Buelita Fe's house we'd walk down the block and attend ten o'clock mass at La Iglesia de San Miguel. I never wanted to go because it was held in Spanish. I understood but I never felt like listening. Instead I'd look up at the ceiling at the yellow glass dome that would glow like a lamp. And when I'd forget where I was it'd be time to kneel. Or stand up. Or kneel down again. Say amen. Why do we have to kneel down and stand up so many times? When it was time for communion Mom would walk to the line at the back where the double doors were. I'd want to go with her so I could move my legs but she'd push me down and say, "Uh-uh, *mija*. You haven't done your communion yet." And I'd act all stupid. "What's that?"

"When you know who *Diosito* is."

Like if I didn't know.

Papi would be dozing off next to me, trying to keep his back straight, and Estrella would be between us, on her knees acting as though she were praying. She hadn't done her communion either, but she was studying for it. She'd been going to Thursday night classes learning the Act of Contrition.

I'd watch Mom walk down the aisle and her curls would bounce and her dress would move like stirring milk. She'd bow her head and move her lips when she stood in front of Padre Félix, then whisper "Amen," open her mouth, and take the wafer. She'd excuse herself to the people in our pew and kneel down next to me, acting all serious, without smiling, like if You were keeping an eye on her. I'd look around and see everyone acting serious, so serious that when it was time to sing they kept their voices down, embarrassed they might be off-key.

I'd pull on Mom's dress but she wouldn't move. Her elbows would be on the back of the pew in front of her and her forehead would be resting on her knuckles. Her eyes would be closed and her lips would hardly move. Sometimes I wondered if she were praying because of something she'd done to Papi. Or something he'd done to her. Or maybe she felt bad for calling him names or for hitting him with something she grabbed from the kitchen drawer. I wanted to let her know that it was okay and that You'd understand. I pulled on her dress but she reached out and pinched me without even looking. I didn't even know what happened, but I remember my skin burning and thinking how much I hated her. I called her names and stuck out my tongue when she wasn't looking even though You were right there between us. But I only hated her for as long as I could feel the sting on my arm.

Tencha once told me we should be careful of what we think and do because You see us better than we see ourselves. Sometimes You find a way inside us to show us who we really are. But you have to let him in, she says. You have to open your heart.

After a lot of kneeling and praying *misa* would end and everyone would walk out the front doors, giving anyone they passed a handshake. Estrella would hold Mom's hand with her chin up like if we were about to take pictures.

Outside, if it wasn't raining, people would give thanks to Padre Félix like if he were some movie star. There'd be a crowd waiting to grab his hands, and Papi would give thanks to him too, but then he'd wait on the side and I'd stand next to him, smelling his sleeve, waiting to leave. Sometimes Mom would make me go give thanks. And I would, because I had to.

But then, we'd all walk to Buelita Fe's, and she'd say

the *sopita* was ready. Pancho would puff up his chest and tell us about the spices he used to rub over the steaks we were going to eat. I'd start to hear the clicks of beer cans going off every few minutes from my *tíos* sitting by the garage, under the patio, and the voices of my cousins running around the house, chasing each other. And after we were done eating fajitas and frijoles and *elote*, we'd sit at the long table made of three other tables pushed together. Some of us on stools, some of us in chairs. We'd take out the jar of pinto beans and bottle caps and loose change so we could play *Lotería*. We'd lay out the *tablas* and choose the ones we wanted. Some of us with two, some of us with four. We'd play a round and fill a vertical line, then a horizontal, two diagonals making an X. And then the corners. *Las Esquinas*. And once we were crowded around the table with our necks stretched to see the pile of cards being dealt, *La Chalupa*, *El Pescado*, *El Cazo*, we'd play a round of blackout. And by then the game would've gotten faster and louder and it'd be hard to keep up with the images stacking up in the middle of the table. Whoever was dealing would throw them down and sing the riddles and someone would miss a card. They'd scream, "Wait! Slow down, *chingao*! What was the last one?" But we'd keep going. We'd play until the sun outside didn't even seem bright anymore, until one of us had everyone else's money, a bulge of quarters and nickels and dimes kept in a Ziploc bag, where it was kept until the following Sunday, when we'd take out our *tablas* and bottle caps and loose change, and do it all over again.

EL PARAGUAS

EL PARAGUAS

I used to run outside when it rained and get so wet it didn't seem like it was raining anymore. I'd run to the back of our neighborhood where there were trails I thought led somewhere. And by the time I came back, I'd be soaked. Mom would rip my clothes off right there in the middle of the kitchen, all mad because she hadn't even known I'd snuck out through our bedroom window.

There was one time Estrella was at the kitchen table drawing or coloring or doing whatever she was doing with paper and scissors. She made a purse out of red construction paper and it opened up like an accordion with a yellow tassel glued at the end. I told her it was pretty, but only a cunt would wear it. Mom turned and looked at me like if I'd dropped a glass. She was wringing my shorts and I was standing there in my underwear, dripping.

"What did you say?" she asked. "Do you know what that means?" I shrugged, but before I dropped my shoulders she slapped me across the face. Not on my cheek but on the side of my eye. I stared at her and she stared at me, like if we were bad actresses in a *telenovela*.

Papi came into the kitchen, *"¿Qué chingado está pasando?"* Estrella had scissors in her hand with the ends pointing up, her mouth was half-open. I didn't know what to do with them looking at me, so I ran out the door and through the yard. I pushed my hair out of my face because I was drowning in it and all I could taste was rain. I heard Papi scream, *"¡Luz! Ven, mija."* But I kept running. I was seven I think, and it was the first time Mom ever hit me.

I could see her face as I ran, the way she looked at me after she hit me. And it didn't hurt and it didn't matter. It was *how* she looked at me. Like if she knew she was wrong and didn't want me to know it. I couldn't understand what her problem was. People said it at school. I was a cunt. She was a cunt. My teacher at school was a cunt. It was like saying *pinche* or *pendejo*. Like when she'd call Papi *un hijo de puta*. There was no reason to slap me just because of a word.

● ● ●

Now it's raining outside and it makes me think of everything that happened because of my hands and these stupid cunt fingers. I could blame them for everything, no? Because if I didn't have fingers or hands maybe none of this would've ever happened.

EL CATRIN

EL CATRIN

Papi would come home from work with black stains on his shirt. I remember him washing his hands at the kitchen sink, scrubbing his knuckles in front of the window. He stopped doing it after awhile and I got used to his hands looking like he'd been working under the hood of a car.

He came home one day wearing a smile that looked like he'd been given an award. He'd been given a promotion as Managing Director of Inventory Planning, which sounded a lot better than steelworker. Mom told us later, when she was tucking us in, that he was going to be assigned to the second floor with a window in his office. The next morning we were going shopping to buy him a suit and a briefcase.

There was one time before then when Papi was watching TV and Mom and Estrella had gone to the supermarket. It was just the two of us and I asked him what he would've wanted to be if he would've gone to school. He said he wanted to be a painter. Not of houses, but an artist. In the garage, there was a painting of his of a waterfall between two mountains and two deer. When we'd clean the garage or take down Christmas decorations from the attic, I'd stare at it. And I never could believe Papi had painted it because it looked so professional.

• • •

He was in the dressing room at Mervyns trying on a navy blue suit for his new promotion and it was like he'd stepped out of a movie. "Where's the sombrero?" I asked. I wanted him to sing. I wanted him to do a two-step. I extended my arms and said, *"¡Ay! Te ves muy caballero."* Estrella brought him ties of different colors and told him how smart he looked. He'd put them on as he wiggled his toes under his socks, then stood in front of the mirror wearing his silly smile. Our faces would peek out from the sides of his back checking to see what a Managing Director looked like.

We didn't mention anything about the promotion to the Silvas that weekend. We went to *misa*, ate lunch, played *Lotería*, then drove home. Papi kept grabbing a section of the newspaper that night even though he'd already looked through it. He'd walk to the garage and come back again. Before I went to bed I gave him a hug.

"*¿Qué?*" he said. "You never do that."

• • •

When I got home from school the following day, Mom called.

"He didn't get it," she said. Just like that. Like if he'd forgotten to pick up cereal on his way home.

"What?"

"He didn't get it, Luz."

She was on the other side of the interstate helping someone put together a piñata for a *posada*. She wasn't getting home until later and said it didn't work out because they changed their minds. Maybe it was his English. She didn't know. "Just be nice. Don't say anything. Act normal." I hung up knowing that at any minute he'd walk through the door, and I didn't know what to do. I thought of going to Tencha's to help her with the tamales she had to make, but I went to my room instead. When he came home I pretended to be asleep.

• • •

That weekend when we played *Lotería* with the Silvas, Papi did something he'd never done before. When you call the cards you sing the riddles. That's what makes it different from bingo. It's not as easy as calling out numbers because in *Lotería* you have to figure out *el dicho* to figure out the image. Either that or keep your eyes on the cards being thrown by the dealer. But the faster the riddles, the faster the game.

Papi got up and dealt the cards. At first his voice was

off-key, and you could tell he was nervous. But he got stronger the more we played.

¡Don Ferruco en la alameda, su bastón quería tirar!
   —(El Catrin)
¡Para el sol y para el agua!—(El Paraguas)
¡El que con la cola pica, le dan una paliza!—(El Alacrán)

Los dichos. Everyone knows them from church fairs and parties. But there's some that people make up for fun. Like *La Sirena.* Tío Fernando would whistle when she was called because she's topless, and Pancho Silva, who normally dealt the cards, would say, *"¡La encuerada para el Tío Fernando!"* And for *El Venado*, he'd sing, *"¡Lo que el Tío José mata cada fin de semana!"* Because Papi liked to go hunting.

But the day Papi dealt, I hadn't known he knew the riddles because I'd never heard him deal, just like I'd never known he wanted to be a painter.

He started singing *los dichos* and they sounded like songs he'd learned from when he was a boy. I couldn't keep up with the game because he was singing so fast, so loud. Pancho kept bringing him beers, making him louder. And when I saw him next to Papi I thought, he's no movie star. He's no Pedro Infante. But look at Papi! He's handsome. He's good-looking. With his chin up and his voice loud. *He's* a movie star. I sat there and looked at him and I didn't even try to play the game, because I couldn't. I couldn't keep up. So I started to clap, in my head, softly at first, then louder and louder until someone called out: *¡Lotería!*

9

EL BARRIL

EL BARRIL

You could say I looked Indian and she looked *gringa*. At school the teachers would ask Estrella if she was Spanish, like from Spain, because of her eyes. "Are they hazel?" Every time I caught her telling teachers she was Spanish I'd walk up to her in the hallway, between classes, with my finger in her face and say, *"¡Hey! ¡Te llamas Castillo!"* But real Mexican and in front of everyone.

Estrella lived in Reynosa for two years after she was born, before moving to the States. Then I arrived, the natural-born out of all of us, which is weird because I'm the one who looks more Mexican.

We used to visit Buelo Fermín and Tío Carlos in Reynosa during the summer, but there we had to speak in Spanish. The only place I could speak comfortably was in my head. We'd sit with Buelo Fermín in his kitchen and nod our heads, and when Estrella would say something I'd wait for her to trip over a sentence. She never spoke Spanish at home so I thought she'd make mistakes. But she spoke like everyone else, smooth and easy.

I understood everyone but was too shy to say anything because I didn't want to sound stupid. I'd lose my words if I spoke. When Buelo Fermín asked me a question, I'd answer him in English. Then he'd throw his shoulders back. He'd point to me and say with his eyes half shut, *"No te olvides de dónde vienes."*

Like if I would forget.

But still, I wouldn't speak to him in Spanish. And so in Reynosa, I was the one who never opened her mouth. If Buelo Fermín spoke to me in Spanish, I'd speak to him in English. It seemed fair. I never paid attention to him anyway. Most of the time I looked at his bruised toes sticking out of his *chanclas*.

• • •

The girls we played with in Reynosa were our age. They liked to run to the market down the block and come back with fruit smothered in lime juice and cayenne pepper. And when I saw them I joined them. Sometimes we'd spray each other with a hose from someone's backyard or sit on the sidewalk and draw shapes on the pavement with chalk. We'd make sounds between us that didn't even make sense: *¡Aye! ¡Onda! ¡Bofos!* And if they wanted to play chase, I'd run after them. If they wanted to play cards, I'd deal. If they wanted to kick a ball, I'd kick it so far they'd disappear around the block before finding it.

One girl had a barrel in her backyard filled with water and there was a game we played where we'd stand around it and dodge torpedoes with our hands. It was dumb, but whoever's turn it was would splash someone and by the end we were all soaked and laughing. Estrella would look at me like if I were some wet dog and say, "You're gonna get it when Mom sees you."

But I'd roll my eyes and say, "No English, remember?"

• • •

We'd go to church by the *plaza de San Pedro* and Papi and Mom would say hi to everyone who still remembered them, because Reynosa was where they first met.

When it happened, Mom had walked into a bakery where Papi was working and ordered *galletas de boda*. When he told me the story he said she was the most beautiful thing he'd ever seen. He thought she was American because of how light her skin was, or from Venezuela. Anywhere but Reynosa. He gave her a box of cookies and told her there was a really good movie playing at *el cine*. But she didn't respond, not at first, and so he gave her another box of cookies. And that's when she smiled, with the second box.

He introduced himself: *José Antonio, señorita. Un placer.* He bowed and grabbed her hand and kissed it.

Jose Antonio Castillo.

Then she smiled and said, *"Cristina. Me llamo Cristina."*

EL APACHE

EL APACHE

Somos iguales, mama," Tencha says to me. "We don't do anything but follow our hearts."

But sometimes she's grumpy, and I wonder if it's because she's not following her own. Or if it's because she's never been married or because her hair is gray and she doesn't color it. Whenever I get close to her I notice the whiskers on her chin. But when she looks at me I can see how much she loves me. She calls me her life, *su vida*. She hasn't found a man to spend her life with and deep down I think she's lonely, even though she says she doesn't need anyone to make her happy.

Mom used to say she didn't get along with Tencha. She couldn't figure out why and there was no good reason, but they just didn't see eye to eye. And that's why Estrella argued with Tencha all the time. She liked acting like she was white and I think it bothered Tencha. She had dark skin like me and Papi, and she reminded Estrella that even though she wasn't dark she was still Mexican. Estrella would tell me how much she hated her and call her *una pinche gorda*. *Una india,* like those women in the streets selling baskets and bracelets.

Tencha would speak softer to her after that. Because of course it hurt her feelings. How can you call someone fat and not expect them to get hurt? Her eyes would get red and she'd explain to Estrella that she thought her manners were not like those of a young lady. But Estrella wouldn't listen. Later in our room she'd tell me how funny it was when Tencha got all serious, and that's when I wanted to hit her.

There've been times when Tencha's called my name and I haven't felt like going to her. But I go to her anyway, and she's sitting on the couch with her arms open, like she's ready to squeeze the life out of me. *"Mira quién es,"* she says. Then I'm covered in her. We sway back and forth, back and forth like on a boat, and she says again, *"Mira quién es, mira quién está conmigo."*

29

EL TAMBOR

EL TAMBOR

The throbbing went through my arms and down my legs and through my veins and back up again into my chest. We had come back from Reynosa a few weeks earlier and Memo had already blown up his hand. I was sitting in front of the television. Papi yanked me away from the couch and dragged me by my hair into the kitchen with his veins coming out from around his nose. You would think Memo wouldn't have said anything, but maybe he did, maybe it slipped. Maybe Tío Carlos told

Papi I'd given Memo a blow job. But I didn't. I didn't put anything in my mouth. I touched him and that was it.

Sometimes the bones in my hand beat from the inside like they did that night and I can remember the moment it broke, when Papi told me to bang my hand against the wall, like in *Nosotros los pobres*, after Pedro Infante slaps Chachita across the face. He bangs his hand against the wall until it bleeds, until it breaks, and she screams, *"¡No! ¡No, Papi! ¡No hagas eso!"*

"¡Fuerte!" Papi yelled. *"¡Dale chingasos!"*

He stood over me and everything looked like it was behind water. Mom ran into the kitchen from the hallway, kind of dumb, not knowing what to do or what was going on. Estrella ran to our room looking at me from the doorway before she turned the corner. Mom tried to stop Papi from grabbing my arm but he pushed her away and started saying what I'd done. He screamed that I'd grabbed *su pinche cosa*. He looked at me and yelled, *"¿Y qué hiciste?"* He wanted me to say it. He wanted me to confess. "What did you do? *¿Qué hiciste?"* He called me *putita*. "Is that what you are? *¿Una putita? ¿Eh? Pégale,* *chingada madre. ¡Ándale!*" He screamed that I jacked him off, my own cousin, my own hand. Seven fucking years old! And I had to learn a lesson. *"¡Pégale! ¡Ándale!"* He grabbed my elbow and banged my hand against the wall. Mom stepped in between us but he slapped her so hard she fell over the counter. We were standing next to the backdoor and the steps that went down to the backyard. I remember the wind coming in making the screen door hit against the frame. Papi pushed me against the wall, and when I stood up he pushed me again toward the door. I fell down the stairs and caught myself on the concrete outside. That's when I noticed my hand dangling from my wrist like an animal hanging off a branch. I grabbed it with my other hand, trying to hold it up. Mom ran out holding her face, and I could see Estrella peeking from our bedroom window that looked out into the backyard. Papi, grabbing his hair with his fists, didn't look like himself anymore.

We got in the truck and drove to the hospital next to the highway. But the throbbing didn't stop and I could hear the beating in my ears. It didn't stop in the waiting room or when the doctor looked at it, or when they wrapped it and told us to come back the following day so they could fix it. It didn't stop until later, much later, after I closed my eyes and passed out from whatever they gave me to kill the pain.

6

LA SIRENA

LA SIRENA

Whenever *La Sirena* was called, I'd look at her above the water with her arms down by her side and her long, wavy hair, wishing I was her. Not because she was pretty or grown-up but because wherever she lived nothing and no one could touch her and she could swim wherever she wanted.

I waited until everyone was inside, always at night when they were sitting on the couch watching late-night television at Tencha's house. She lived a block away from us. I'd wrap two towels around my legs and overlap them to cover my feet, then tie string from my ankles to my knees before rolling into her pool from the shallow end. It was a shitty pool that came with the house she rented, but it was five feet deep and enough to get lost in. The towels would soften around my legs and the extra material that fell over my feet would feel like the fins from a goldfish. I'd wiggle from one side of the pool to the other, humming a song with my eyes wide open, not knowing whether I was crying or not because I was underwater, and I'd dare myself to stay there for as long as I could.

EL BORRACHO

EL BORRACHO

None of us knew how to play instruments. I took guitar lessons for a year but quit because my teacher smelled like tomato soup. Estrella liked to sing but when she'd open her mouth Papi said there was no use in trying because she didn't have a good ear. Mom would sing Rocío Durcal when she was cleaning the house or making dinner, and sometimes Papi would join her, singing the part of Juan Gabriel in "Déjame vivir." Together they'd sing, moving their shoulders and blowing kisses at each other—*¡Así es que déjame y vete ya!*

But if I heard *cumbia*, especially Selena, then I'd start dancing. When we were at wedding receptions everyone on the dance floor would stand back in a circle and cheer me on. At home I'd turn up the volume and make up dances in the middle of the living room with the coffee table pushed against the wall. I'd drag Estrella from the kitchen and ask her to be my partner, but she said she couldn't because she had two left feet. She was either flipping through magazines or writing notes to her friends.

There was a movie about a girl who wanted to be a dancer and I learned the solo that came at the end. I ran to the front yard wanting to do the gymnastic moves, but then I was too chicken to try them, even on the grass.

When Papi sang in the backyard I'd dance to whatever song he sang. He'd be a little drunk under the light of the porch, and for every four sips he took, I took one. I'd put on one of Mom's aprons too big for me and grab it with my hands, then throw it back and to the sides like a flamenco dancer, like Lola Flores. I'd mouth the words. *"¡Otra, hombre!"* the way she does and Papi would laugh because I was acting grown-up, pretending to be Lola

Flores with my lips pushed together. None of the neighbors cared about the noise. On one side there was an old couple short as midgets and partly deaf, so it didn't matter. And on the other side there was a younger couple without any kids. I caught the lady who lived there peeking at us from a window one night, but she didn't say anything. Maybe she liked the music. Maybe she was mouthing the words. We were all Mexican in Magnolia Park.

Papi and I sang and danced until I got dizzy. Then later, in bed, in some dream, I'd be black and white, all grown-up with brown hair and big lips, dancing in the middle of all these men and women watching me, playing their instruments, guitars, accordions, and trumpets, singing, *"¡Olé! ¡Olé!"* And my hands would be on my hips and my chest would be out. My lips pushed together like Lola Flores.

53

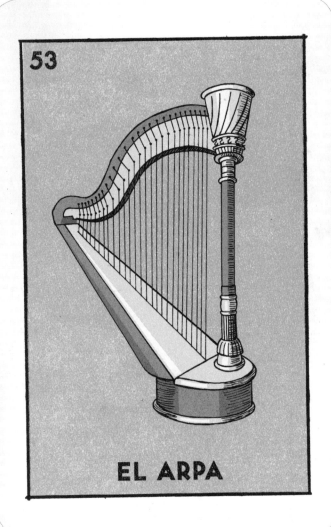

EL ARPA

EL ARPA

They used to pinch me when I'd say something wrong. Not a bad word, not a *maldición*. Just a word that came before another, one that turned something into either a woman or a man. *La* something or *El* something. As if the moon weren't Romeo one night and Juliet another.

They'd pinch me if I called something a boy instead of a girl, or the other way around. Why is it *la mano* instead of *el mano*? I can think of Papi's hands and think they're masculine, then think of Mom's and think they're feminine. If we were talking about the hands of a clock it could go either way. The hands of a clock could be bi.

Once I asked Estrella what a bisexual was and she glared at me like if I'd asked her if she'd ever kissed a boy. "Where did you hear about bisexuals?" she asked. "Where did you?" I asked. "From Angélica, she told me Luis Miguel is bisexual. That he spends time with women in front of cameras but at night in hotel rooms he spends time with *hombres*." "What!" "Yeah," she said. "He's gay!"

"But you just said he's bisexual."

Why isn't a harp female? I've only seen the one in *Lotería*. Every time we play on Sundays at Buelita Fe's house they give me a chance to deal, and so when it comes I throw it down on the table and call it out with confidence, *"¡La Arpa!"* But Estrella laughs at me, and then everyone else does too.

"Why is everyone laughing?"

Papi says to me, as if he's my guidance counselor, *"El arpa, mija.* Not *La arpa."*

"How are you supposed to know?" I ask them.

They say the same thing all the time, that if a word

ends in "a" it's probably a feminine word. And if it ends in anything else it's masculine. But that's not always the case. Sometimes a word that ends in "a" is masculine, and other times, it's feminine. How am I supposed to know what is woman and what is man simply by the arrangement of letters? It's like at school when they teach you the rules of how to speak, then later teach you how to break those rules. Like you can't say, "Look what the cat drug in." You say, "Look what the cat dragged in." Stupid verbs, stupid rules. But the point you're trying to make is there, right there in front of you as you stand and stare at it. Pointing. *La luna*. *El luna*.

The moon!

14

LA MUERTE

LA MUERTE

I didn't go to breakfast today so by nine-thirty there was a knock on the door. I didn't answer but the door opened and Julia's head popped in. "What are you doing?" she asked. "What does it look like I'm doing, *pendeja*?" That's what I wanted to say, but I didn't. I was at my desk with the *Lotería* deck in front of me and *La Muerte* turned over. My journal was tucked under my mattress, but I was trying to think of what to write. I turned to her and opened my hands, like if to say, "What the hell do you think?"

Then she closed the door.

• • •

After the bones shattered I had a cast on my arm for about a month and a half. I was supposed to cover it with a plastic bag when I showered, and I did, but it got wet anyway, and when it dried it itched and so I pulled the cotton out from inside.

When the doctor, Dr. Roberto, took it off he said it had never happened before. He asked me if I took care of it the way I was supposed to. I told him, yes, I'd taken care of it the way I was supposed to. He threw his clipboard on the counter and picked it up and threw it down again. My wrist was dislocated. He'd put it back in place when he'd put the cast on but now it was too late. I hadn't taken care of it the way I was supposed to and there was no way to fix it. I was just going to have to live with a dislocated wrist. He said all of this to Mom, not me, even though I was standing right there next to her.

I grew a lot of hair on my arm during the time I had the cast on. Once it came off my skin was white. But I was happy I didn't have it on anymore. The first thing I did was grab a pen and write my name. To make sure I could write at least. I looked at him and said it was fine. I didn't care if it was dislocated.

I wanted to leave, but Dr. Roberto started talking to Mom. So I went to the waiting room and there were those children's magazines, *Highlights*, with the games in the back where you have to find hidden objects in a picture. I did all of them, and when I was done they were still talking in the hallway. I heard laughter. When I looked over she was standing up straight and pulling her shirt down so it'd look ironed. In the car I asked her what they were talking about.

"I think I just got a job."

The way she said it, maybe it was her face, maybe it was how excited she seemed. She hadn't had a job. It wasn't that she couldn't speak English. She spoke fine, better than Papi, but it never came up, her having a job. Now she was going to work for Dr. Roberto, the man who said I didn't take care of my wrist the way I was supposed to.

"How did he know you needed a job?" We were listening to María Castro on the radio. I remember because I thought Mom looked like her, the way she was driving, her back off the seat, leaning forward. She looked like María Castro. She said they were talking and she mentioned that she didn't have a job, and now on top of the house bills she had to pay medical expenses. That's when he offered. He told her she could clean his house.

"Did he give it to you at the beginning or at the end?"

"What do you mean *give?*"

"After you were laughing or before?"

"What do you mean laughing, Luz?"

"I saw you laughing. I heard you."

"He told me right before I left. He gave me his number and said I could start next week."

"You're going every day?"

"Not every day. Maybe three times a week."

"Where does he live?"

"Somewhere on the south side, past the highway. He

said he has a garden and doesn't have time to take care of it."

"A garden?"

"Yes, Luz, a garden!"

There was a hat she never wore on the floor of the passenger side, made of white straw with a blue ribbon around it. I grabbed it and put it on, pulled the top down over my eyes and thought of Dr. Roberto's "garden." I could see Mom clipping whatever bushes and plants he had. The sun beating down on her skin. The droplets of sweat sliding down her face. And Dr. Roberto calling her from the back door, "Cristina, come inside. Take a break. Have a cold drink with me." Mom turning around, her back straight, looking like María Castro.

11

EL MELÓN

EL MELÓN

Papi would go hunting on weekends and ask me if I wanted to go with him. He'd grab the rifle from under his mattress, where he kept it, and take me to the backyard so I could practice. "Hold it like this," he'd say, with his right arm wrapped around it. He'd point to the melons on a stump against the fence at the far end of the backyard and say, "Shoot like if it were the head of something you hate."

The rifle was too big. When I'd wrap my arms around it Estrella would stare at me like if I were a jackass. But eventually I found my way, which wasn't the way I was supposed to do it. Instead of holding it with my arms I tried holding it against my body. But when I pulled the trigger the force knocked me down. And when I put my cheek against the butt, so that I could look at the pointer and center my aim on a melon against the fence, it'd knock me down. My cheek would puff up like if I'd been punched, and Papi would laugh and help me up, telling me to try again. *"Ándale, otra vez."*

I had to keep my legs open. That's what it was.

"Keep your elbows up *también*," he said. But the rifle would slip out when I did that. It was too heavy, and the only way I could do it was if I held it against my body, so that it'd become a part of me. I had to push into it. And when I figured that out, all of a sudden those melons exploded. The pins and needles in my fingers were nothing compared with being knocked down. I learned to lean into it and not pull away. Pushing into it is what kept me from getting hurt.

But there you go. That's how it is.

51

LA PALMA

LA PALMA

My arms and legs were open like a star facing the sun. That's how I used to lie under the tree when Mom was cleaning the house and Papi was either working on the truck or mowing the yard. Back then my hair was long, down to my waist, and for some reason, the bangs around my face were always curly like a bad perm. I'd try to comb it after I came out of the shower, but when it dried it would bunch up. So I just let it run wild and do whatever it wanted. Estrella would comb it down and I'd have to use my neck muscles to keep my head straight. Mom said

I should let it be, that maybe when I got older it would unravel. Maybe when I got older I wouldn't seem all over the place. "I'm not all over the place," I'd tell her. But she said I was. She'd say sometimes I was easy because I was quiet, but sometimes I wasn't because I wanted attention. And if no one gave me attention I'd keep bothering them until they'd listen. *Muy cabezona*, she'd say, like your father. Stubborn as a mule.

But whatever.

17

EL BANDOLÓN

EL BANDOLÓN

Mom used to say Pancho Silva had a good ear but I remember them the size of waffle fries. His voice sounded rough and broken, and if he started telling us a story it would take him forever to shut up. Like when he'd tell us about Pedro Infante or how someone discovered him as an actor in Mexico City. He was drinking at a bar in the middle of the day taking a break from a job at a creamery. A woman in a red suit with a bun over her head the size of a pomegranate noticed him. She told him he looked like Pedro Infante, that the similarity was remarkable. Even the build was the same.

From then on Pancho started working as Pedro Infante's double.

But then Pedro died. He was in a plane crash, somewhere in the mountains, and it took them a long time to find the pieces of the plane because they were lost under trees. The search patrol never found the metal plate that was inside Pedro's head from a previous surgery. So of course, people think he's still alive, hiding in a cave somewhere. Life as a movie star was too much for him. The story of the plane crash was a way to be left alone.

Pancho said Pedro would visit him in Magnolia Park in the middle of the night, and he'd tell him that he was living in a small town outside of Puerto Vallarta. They'd sit on the porch and talk in the dark and strum the strings of a guitar until morning, then Pedro would say good-bye and tiptoe out through the front gate.

None of us believed him.

Gastón would ask, "Really, Pancho? Pedro Infante was here last night and you didn't take a picture?" He explained why taking a picture would've been a bad idea. If someone found out Pedro was alive and in Magnolia Park his cover would've been blown. It'd be on the cover of a magazine like *National Enquirer*.

"*Cállate ya, Papa,*" Tío Daniel would say, and Pancho would storm out waving his hands in the air. He'd go to the back patio where his barbecue pit was, because that's where he went to calm himself. Tío Daniel would say he was losing his mind, already at sixty-eight years old, and he felt sorry for him.

42

LA CALAVERA

LA CALAVERA

Estrella was in the kitchen with Mom: "I could have two tiers on both sides, all white with stairs and the tiara on top, but not on the cake. I want it next to the music box." "You want the music to be playing the whole time?" "Yeah, the whole time." "And if no one can hear it?" "Maybe we could put a small microphone somewhere?"

I was in the living room with Papi, watching, but not really watching, the news. We weren't talking to each other. I can't remember why, but I think it was because we had gone hunting the day before and my wrist was sore from pulling the trigger. When I complained about my wrist and fingers he always thought I was throwing it in his face, because of the accident. But I wasn't throwing it in his face. It was true, sometimes it was hard to move my fingers, especially my thumb, because it felt stuck.

From nowhere a smell came inside the house, a horrible smell, like something had died. Papi and I turned our heads and looked out the window because it was coming from there.

Estrella and Mom came into the living room with their faces all twisted.

Papi said a *pinche perro* must've died. He got up and walked to the window.

"It's true. It smells like something died," I said.

All four of us went to the windowsill, shoulder to shoulder, and looked out, like if the bad smell was riding a horse and we wanted to see it pass. Like if we wanted to point to it and say, "Look! *¡Allí esta!*" Then it would make sense. Because it'd be something we could see.

But then, *¡Bofos!* It was gone.

Our heads were out the window and all we could smell was the ordinary air. We looked like dogs ourselves with our noses out, sniffing and trying to find that horrible stink. It was the weirdest thing.

Papi sat back down and grabbed the remote. Mom and Estrella went back to the kitchen and Estrella continued planning her *Quinceañera*. It was four years away, but already she was planning on becoming a young lady.

22

LA BOTA

LA BOTA

There was one day people from church were supposed to come over for lunch. Mom had been cutting tomatoes and browning meat, making rice. I thought we were going to skip breakfast because of the small plates filled with diced onions and cilantro. "When are they coming?" I asked. She shrugged and said, "They'll come when they come." But she said it like if there was something she wasn't telling me.

"Is something wrong?" I asked.

"No, I'm fine!" she said.

"Then why are you wearing those shoes?" I said. "You wear those only when you dress up."

"We're having company. Okay? Is that all right with you?"

But company never came. The diced onions dried up and the meat got cold. We sat on the couch like if we were waiting for the dentist. When we got hungry we had Frosted Flakes even though there was food on the table, and then around three we had tacos while Mom started to clean. She kept walking in front of the television, picking up the junk mail lying around, while the three of us just sat there, not helping. She asked Papi to mow the lawn but he said he'd do it later.

"Mom?" I said.

"What?"

"Te quiero."

She walked to the kitchen and kept cleaning, putting things away acting like she didn't hear me, then grabbed her purse and said she'd forgotten to do a few rooms at Dr. Roberto's house. She might as well do them, she said. Then she was gone. Papi stood up and watched her from the window get in her car and leave. He stood with his hands on his hips.

"She didn't change her shoes?" I said.

"What?"

"Her boots. She's didn't change her boots."

And he acted like he didn't hear me.

36

EL CAZO

EL CAZO

Julia says the same thing every time, about Papi and the family and needing to know more so they can help him. In a few days the district attorney will make a decision, so if there's anything I want to tell them I should tell them now. "Luz? Do you feel like talking?"

I walked away from her and came to my desk and flipped the top card to see what *dicho* I'd make up next.

Write it down, mama. *Échale ganas*.

• • •

Yesterday, a black dress was on the door when I woke up.

I hadn't fallen asleep until three because I stayed up writing. Usually by ten in the morning I'm either in the common room watching game shows or flipping through a book. Sometimes I watch Mexican films on Univision. Mom would've probably wanted me to read Spanish books, but I've never liked them. When I've tried to read one I get to the bottom of a page and don't even know what I'm reading.

Tencha said the funeral would be at La Iglesia de San Miguel, and afterward we'd go to the cemetery near Pasadena Mall. They're taking Estrella back to Mexico to bury her there, and so going to the cemetery is just pretend. She had to call Buelo Fermín in Reynosa because she didn't have enough money, and he told her that there was a spot for Estrella in Mexico, planned a long time ago. There's a spot for me too.

I didn't like the dress she brought me. It had white lace with a thick glossy belt and was long enough to reach my feet. I left it on the bed and went to the bathroom and showered for a long time, so long it was the longest I've ever been in there. I pushed the shower head away from me and lathered myself with Ivory soap while steam fogged the mirror. I rubbed between my toes and under my armpits, everywhere I never usually clean, because I wanted to be clean. I had black jeans and a black shirt that had a touring schedule for a Selena concert on the back. But the front was solid black.

"Uh-uh, mama," Tencha said when I opened the door. She was sitting on one of the chairs against the wall in the hallway, with a black shawl over her head. "You're not going dressed like that."

I motioned toward the front door.

"Mama! *¡Por favor!* You're not going like that." She opened her hands like if she wanted me to take off my clothes and give them to her.

I waited for her to stand up.

On the way out Larry said good-bye and reminded us that I had to be back before seven. He was sorry, but it was the rules. I didn't see Julia anywhere. I thought she'd walk us to the car and act like some caregiver or something. But I didn't see her. It was Saturday.

They let Tencha take me in her car, even though there was an officer following us the whole time. I stared out the window and wanted to ask if we could go somewhere else, to Astroworld or the Galleria. I didn't want to see anyone that would make me feel like if I were carrying bricks in my pockets.

It didn't hit me until we were in Magnolia Park, near our old house, that I'd see the Silvas. That they probably knew everything that happened. I thought of Buelita Fe and felt sick. When we passed a McDonald's I pointed to it and tried to get Tencha to stop. But she said no. We couldn't be late. She didn't know what had gotten into me.

The parking lot was half-full when we got there. On the way inside I stepped into a puddle because I was staring at a house across the street, at a black Doberman sleeping near the front steps.

Tencha grabbed me by the hand and pulled me toward the entrance. There was hardly anyone inside except for the Silvas and a few neighbors I recognized. At the altar, behind Padre Félix, was the coffin, closed with white roses over it. I wanted to sit behind everyone, but Tencha kept walking, pulling me forward. We passed the pews and I kept my head down. As soon as we sat in the first row I heard those words, *"En el nombre del Padre, del Hijo, del Espíritu Santo, Amen."*

Then everyone stood up.

The last time I'd been there I was sitting in our usual spot, on the left side about ten pews back. I turned my head, because I wanted to see if we were still there: Mom, Papi, Estrella, and me. But Buelita Fe was there, staring at me and grabbing her elbows like if she were hugging herself.

The whole time I felt like if she were next to me. Because she could've been. So what if she was, kneeling and praying the way she used to when Mom would get up and take communion. I wanted to hear her voice. But all I could hear was Padre Félix and the organ in the corner behind him.

Maybe she had nothing to say to me.

I stayed close to Tencha after communion because I didn't want to talk to anyone. They'd want to know how I was doing or tell me how sorry they were. They'd tell me that things happen. Accidents happen. Or maybe they wouldn't say anything at all.

When we were outside, Tía Hilda tried to get me to look at her, but I kept my head down and looked at my shoes, my black Adidas with the word SAMBA on them. Buelita Fe was the only one that didn't push me. She grabbed my hand and patted it, then wiped my face like if it was dirty, and now it was clean. When I smelled her dishwashing soap on her hands, it was like my insides started folding and I started crying, keeping my mouth shut so they wouldn't hear me.

In the car on our way back to the center I wanted to tell Tencha I was sorry for not wearing the dress she bought me. I was sorry I didn't want to go to the cemetery or the reception. But all I wanted was to go see Papi. She kept driving and looking forward like if there was nothing else to do but go back to the center.

Then I said something, something stupid that came to my mind. It was the first time I opened my mouth since it happened. The first time I said anything.

"Why don't we go back to Mexico?"

She paused for a moment, looking at me then back at the road. I guess she needed a moment to realize that I'd spoken. She tried not to make a big deal about it. Like if she knew all along it would come. "I love you. *Lo sabes, ¿verdad?*"

"Yeah," I said.

"But why would you say that?"

"Because." I looked at her and wiped my face.

"You want to go to school in Mexico and leave your Papi? Is that what you want? I love you. You know that, right? But you don't want to go back to Mexico," she said. "It's better for you here."

I looked down at my lap with my palms over my thighs. "It doesn't mean I don't love her," I said.

"I know, mama," she said. "I know."

32

EL MÚSICO

EL MÚSICO

There was a singing competition on *Siempre en Domingo* for kids. We were sitting around the television at Buelita Fe's one weekend, rooting for the ones we thought should win. Some of them came out wearing dresses like holiday decorations. They shimmied their shoulders and couldn't sing to save their lives, but because they were show-offs they got a lot of applause. One little boy came out dressed as a mariachi and sang a Tony Aguilar song, singing as strong as a rooster with a voice that got everyone's attention. Buelita Fe said she'd seen an interview with him earlier that day, and his name was Federico. He was from a town in the middle of nowhere and was real poor. This was his big chance. His mother and father asked the church for money so he could get to *Siempre en Domingo* for the competition. In the interview he said, "This is for my mother and father, because we don't have any money. We only have one bed. If I win, I'll work hard because I want us to move out of our small house. I want to buy my father a truck so he doesn't have to take the bus anymore. And maybe on weekends, we can go to the beach." Buelita Fe was crying by the time she finished telling us.

I looked at Papi and asked, "Why is she crying?"

"Because," he said. "She cries at everything."

"But what's so sad about that? He's good, he's probably going to win."

"He wants to buy his father a truck. And he wants to go to the beach."

"That's why she's crying?"

"Yeah, that's why."

I listened to that boy sing. He stood with his arms

down next to him and looked out to the audience with his eyes full of everything his mom and dad had taught him. When he was almost done, singing his last note, making a face like if he were trying to lift a car, I felt something light up inside of me. Not because he was poor or because he wanted to go to the beach but because his voice was so strong it pressed in the middle of my chest. When the song finished, Buelita Fe dried her cheeks with a bunched-up tissue she'd been holding the entire competition.

47

LA CORONA

LA CORONA

Mom was the last one to close the door, looking over her shoulder, as if to remind me, "That's what you get for being *una chiflada*."

I didn't want to play with Estrella's friends anyway. It was her birthday party. She turned twelve and all the presents were for her.

I was on my third cheeseburger when I saw the man walk in. He had a gym bag over his shoulder with red Bozo shoes on. He walked straight to the bathroom in the back of the restaurant, and ten minutes later he came out as Ronald

McDonald with white makeup on and a red afro. When he passed me, he winked and said, "Our secret, right?"

I could see the stubble under his white makeup and he smelled like bacon. He thought I was playing along, but really, I didn't care. He leaned over and asked who the birthday girl was. I looked outside. Estrella and her friend Angélica were swinging on a chained tire. Other kids were running around, screaming, "You're it! You're it!" Mom and her friends were sitting in their hips, looking at the highway. A girl with thick glasses sitting at the end of the monkey bars reminded me of La Chilindrina from *El chavo del ocho*, except she didn't have any freckles. She lived on Market, in a red house that didn't look like the others. Estrella didn't hang out with her and neither did I. I don't know how she was invited. Mom probably told her, because she wanted us to be friends with her.

Chilindrina was looking at us. I took a bite from my cheeseburger and pointed at her. With my mouth full I said, "The girl with the glasses."

Ronald McDonald stepped out onto the playground and spread his arms open like an airplane. He had a paper crown around his elbow, gold with ruby stickers on it. Estrella ran toward him but he walked past her and straight to Chilindrina. He took the crown from his arm and placed it over her head and must've said Happy Birthday, or something. He grabbed her with both arms and lifted her off the wooden deck. Mom walked toward him, shaking her hand, while Estrella grabbed the crown and put it on. Then they turned, and he pointed at me.

I ran to the handicapped bathroom and locked the door and waited for an hour before I came out. By then I figured the coast was clear. When I walked out Ronald McDonald was sitting in a booth with his wig on the table. And when I walked past him I stuck out my tongue. "Our secret, right?" I said.

Nothing outside had changed. Everyone was still playing the same games as before.

On the table where I was sitting was the bent, deformed crown that was supposed to be for the birthday girl. I put it on and went outside and climbed the wooden deck, sat down next to Chilindrina and asked her if she'd ever seen *El chavo del ocho*.

41

LA ROSA

LA ROSA

We had rosebushes in the front yard. You'd think it was Mom's idea, but it wasn't. It was Papi's. He wanted rosebushes because they reminded him of *La Virgen de Guadalupe*.

We were drunk and had come back from a wedding reception for Papi's boss's daughter. He told Papi we should go and have a good time because there was going to be a margarita fountain. There wasn't going to be much tequila in it so it was okay. "Your family will have a good time," he said. And when Papi came home and told us we ran to our rooms and got dressed as fast as we could. But he called out and said, "Not now! The wedding's tomorrow."

The following day Estrella put on a dress and wore her white satin shoes. I wore jeans and a shirt. Nothing fancy. When we got there Papi headed straight for the fountain while Mom, Estrella, and I sat at a long table at the end of the room where no one else was sitting. We didn't know anyone and all we wanted was a margarita. I convinced Mom that it was a good idea to have a drink because we had to show respect to the people getting married.

There's always *barbacoa* at weddings and so I asked if I could get some. Mom said okay, but not too much. She reminded me to watch my manners.

I nodded but then grabbed two paper plates and piled it with frijoles, *arroz*, tortillas, chorizo and *barbacoa*. When I got back to the table Papi had four margaritas in clear plastic cups in his hands with limes hooked on the rim. Mom pushed her lips together like if it was a bad idea, but then took a sip and started dancing with Papi.

In the car on the way home Mom asked us how we felt, but then she laughed and rolled her eyes like if she'd forgotten the question. The car felt like a boat and everything moved twice as much as it should've, but I could still bring everything into focus. It was Estrella who looked like she was going to faint or throw up, and Papi told her to stick her head out the window to get some air. She had drunk three cups, and I had four.

"Como la flor" came on the radio and we started singing real loud, real bad, all together. Out the windows and in each other's faces. We didn't know the words but we made them up and it didn't matter. When the chorus came, we turned into one big voice and screamed so loud we felt each other's breath on our skin. *Ayyyyy, cómo me duele.*

When we got home and pulled into the driveway, like a *borracha*, Estrella got out of the car and ran around the house singing the chorus as loud as she could. She looked stupid and funny with her arms above her head until she ran through the rosebushes, and she didn't even know it, not at first. But I could see it in her eyes. She felt something. Then she touched her face and felt the blood and started screaming like if someone had cut off her hands. All dramatic. I mean, they were just scratches. Mom pulled her into the house, screaming to Papi, *"¡Ya ves! ¡Mira lo que hiciste!"*

Estrella sat on the kitchen table looking up at the light as Mom patted her face with a wet towel. Her dress was spotted with drops of blood, like roses, and it reminded me of the story about *El indio* and *La Virgen de Guadalupe*. She appeared on his poncho a long time ago when no one believed she existed, when no one believed we had our own mother in the sun. She appeared out of nowhere on top of a mountain outside Mexico City and asked *El indio* to collect roses for her, and to take them to the bishop who wanted proof that he'd really seen her and that she was real. When *El indio* carried the roses in his *tilma* to the bishop and released the corners of the fabric, dropping the roses to his feet, there she was on his chest, *La Virgen de*

Guadalupe. It was the first time we knew what she looked like, the first time You gave us a sign. We saw her hands pressed together and her head tilted to the side. And her dark skin. And her soft face. And her almost-closed eyes.

All because of the roses.

7

LA ESCALERA

LA ESCALERA

I used to chase Estrella around the house and hang out in front where the sidewalk is, saying hi to the people who passed by on their way to the supermarket. When I'd get bored, I'd grab the ladder from the garage and climb it to the roof. From there I could look down and see Estrella and all of Magnolia Park. She wouldn't notice me. She'd be wearing her sunglasses and flip through the stations on a portable radio and act like she was a teenager already, like the girls who would pass in their boyfriends' cars, sitting in the passenger side with the window rolled down and their hair pulled back, wearing their bikini for a top. I could tell by the way Estrella looked at them that she hoped they'd notice her and her dark sunglasses she thought were so cool. She'd roll up her tank top so it looked like a bikini, and from the roof of the house I could see the cars passing by and the guys who drove them. They were always bigheaded and lowrider looking, blasting *cumbias* from a piece of shit car that might break into pieces by the time it got to the corner.

After I got bored, I'd climb down the ladder and go inside, lie down on the couch and listen to the fan in front of the window. Mom would either be cleaning or on the phone talking to someone in Mexico.

Papi by then was getting better, but he was still drinking, just not as much.

Around that time there'd been a family talk. Estrella and I were in our room and Mom told us to come to the kitchen. She had two cups of coffee and two cups of Abuelita hot chocolate. "Where's the marshmallows?" I asked, trying to be funny.

"We ran out," she said. "Stop talking and listen."

Papi had just showered and was clean-shaven. He'd combed his hair and was drinking coffee like if it was morning. He told us that he wasn't going to drink any-more. That it wasn't good for him. Mom was sitting next to him, nodding at every word he said.

"It's not good for you," he said. And I thought, *It's not good for you, either.*

But a week or two later, instead of staying in the living room he went to the garage and acted like he was working on his truck. It made funny sounds when he turned it on, but I don't think there was anything wrong with it.

When I went out there to see what he was doing I could smell Don Pedro on him. Sometimes, to be nice, I'd start singing *rancheras* to see if he wanted to sing, but he'd prop open the hood and start checking things like if he was in the middle of something. And because he was in the garage, I couldn't get the ladder and climb to the roof. Because if he saw me he wouldn't let me. But from there I would've been able to see what he was doing, even though I already knew.

40

EL ALACRÁN

EL ALACRÁN

Mom would put on a face when other people were around, like when we'd go to the Silvas or to the supermarket. People would think she was sweet and kind, running errands in the neighborhood with her two daughters. They'd say, "The taller one looks like you," then look at me and not say a word.

We'd go to Kmart and Estrella would get something she wanted, either another pair of colored pencils for the books she liked to draw in or a new pair of pink stockings she might one day use for her *Quinceañera*. I asked for a skateboard once but I didn't get it, even after I asked nicely. We got in the car and Mom turned around and said I was being a pain in the ass. She had a lot of errands to run and if I kept pestering her I was going to make her blow up. She grabbed the steering wheel like if we were about to crash and said, "You want me to blow up?" Sometimes she'd turn around and pinch me, and all that sweetness people thought she was turned into something *picoso*. Papi used to call her *una pinche loca* because when she lost it, she really lost it. And if he called her *una pinche loca* she'd call him *un hijo de puta*. And that would start the fighting.

Papi hated the word *puta* because of that time with Memo, the way he probably saw my hand on his dick even though I'd never touched it because his pants were on the whole time. Papi'd see my face when he'd hear the word *puta* or *putita*, and I think Mom knew that. She'd say it on purpose because it would remind him of me. Then he'd remember how he broke my hand even though it was an accident.

After Mom called him *un hijo de puta* they'd call each

other all the bad things they could think of. He'd grab her wrists and press her down, probably telling himself that she'd shut up if he could only keep her down. And when I'd see him on top of her like that, I could see it in his eyes, the way he looked at her. He didn't want to hit her. He just wanted her to stop fighting. But she'd call him names and hit him across the head and when he couldn't take it anymore he'd use the back of his hand. She'd yell with tears over her cheeks. *"¡Eres un hijo de puta! ¿Me oyes?"*

In the kitchen the next day, she'd be at the stove making eggs, not wanting to turn around. Then finally she'd turn around and we'd see Band-Aids on the sides of her eyes. Estrella would try to help her with the dishes, but she'd brush her away like if she were some fly.

Whenever they'd fight we'd go to our room because it was safer there. Sometimes watching them would make us feel like throwing up. I can't remember the first time it happened but I remember when he knocked over the table and we ran to our room like cockroaches when a light is turned on.

We locked the door and held each other like if we were

waiting for an earthquake, afraid the ceiling might cave-in. A chair would slam against the wall and we'd flinch. Glasses would break. The walls would tremble. They'd scream so loud it felt like wolves were tearing up the house, saying words that didn't even make sense anymore, and the sounds that did come out of their mouths were like dogs.

We'd stand in our room staring at each other until it ended. Because that was the game, to see who could last the longest listening to the furniture being thrown without running away. But there'd be a note in Mom's voice that would mark her breaking point, when she couldn't take it anymore, and the way we could tell was by the sounds being pushed out of her body. Because when he'd kick her in the stomach or hit her across the face they were different kinds of sounds. And when those sounds would alternate, Estrella would lose.

"Let's go," she'd say. Her mouth would tighten and she'd try to hold it in but she'd crawl out of the window and look at me, asking me with her eyes, "What are you doing? Are you stupid?" I'd stand there not saying a word, like a statue, thinking, no, I'm not stupid. I stayed until it was over. Sometimes I'd sit on the floor and deal the cards because looking at the cards would help me forget. I'd tell myself the riddles to keep me from hearing them scream:

The one who dies with a hook in its mouth. *El Pescado*.

A lamp for the ones in love. *La Luna*.

Something identical to the other. *La Bota*.

I stayed in case something happened, in case I'd have to call someone.

After a long stillness, I'd hear them walking around in the living room, neither of them saying anything, putting furniture back where it belonged. The sound of *Three's Company* on television.

One time during the quiet that usually came afterward, I crept into the hallway to check whether or not they'd killed each other, because I couldn't hear them and a long time had passed. But from the hallway I saw Papi holding Mom from behind, leaning over the kitchen table with his hand over her face and her cheeks pulled down. I could see the whites of her eyes and he was banging the table like if he were trying to move it, but it wouldn't move, and I could hear her sighing. It reminded me of when we'd go hunting and have to twist a deer's neck after we shot it in case it hadn't died. Something turned in my stomach and I ran to my room, but even there, with the door closed, and the door locked, I could see him banging her over the table and I wondered if it was my fault, because of that time he'd pushed me down the stairs and I'd broken my hand. Mom said she'd never forgive him for that. And from then on that word *puta* would start everything. I don't remember them fighting before my wrist broke or before Papi called me *putita*. Maybe throwing it in his face was Mom's way of fighting back, defending me somehow. Or maybe she was mad at me because of what I'd done, and she was taking it out on him, blaming him somehow. Or they were taking it out on each other and really they should've been beating me, banging me against the table until I was sighing like a dying dog.

That time I saw them over the table, I crawled out the

window and ran down the street to the corner store and stole pieces of chewing gum and put them all in my mouth at one time. I chewed so fast my cheeks burned, and they burned so much that I told myself I was crying because of the sting, not because they were fighting.

15

LA PERA

LA PERA

Late one night there was a phone call and Papi told us to get dressed and get in the truck. He drove to the hospital near Majestic Harbor and kept saying that Pancho Silva was on the third floor. When the elevators opened, I saw a row of seats at the end of the hallway lit from above with green fluorescent lights. Everyone was there, sitting next to each other with their heads down. Buelita Fe was holding a handkerchief in her hands, twisting it around her fingers, and Gastón stood between Tía Elsa's knees eating a pear like if he were at a picnic. I peeked into the room where Pancho was lying down and saw Tía Hilda holding his hand. It was quiet and no one said a word. I pulled on Mom's sleeve and mouthed, "What's wrong?" She tapped her chest three times. Like if that was supposed to tell me. *"¿El corazón?"* I asked, and she nodded. Luisa made trips back and forth to the vending machines on the first floor, but she never came back with anything.

After awhile, Tía Hilda called everyone into the room. We walked inside looking at the floor, and stood in a semicircle around the bed holding hands. Mom stood behind me and Papi stood behind Estrella. We looked at Pancho and held hands as Tía Hilda said a prayer. His eyes were closed and his head was tilted back like if there were something crawling up his neck.

I don't remember what happened after that because all I can remember is wanting to go home.

● ● ●

After he died I was with Estrella a lot of the time. Neither of us knew what to do or how to act. It was like we both had a secret but we didn't know how to keep it. She'd look through a Sears catalog when we were at home, or cut out pictures from teen magazines while I spent time building a house of cards. Sometimes when I'd build one three stories high, I could hear her go quiet. "Careful, careful," she'd say, as I put another card on top of the house. But always when she looked, it'd fall.

One day I was sitting on the couch watching television. She walked inside from the garage door and, like all the times she came home, I expected her to walk to our room and shut herself in. But she put her backpack down and walked around the couch and sat down next to me. I wasn't sure what she wanted, but she put her arms around me and hugged me for a long time. And we just sat there, like a statue of two girls trying to do the right thing.

EL DIABLITO

EL DIABLITO

Tencha's toes are purple and she has veins the color of green lizards crawling up her legs. Her feet would ache and swell after a day of walking in the market on Alexander Street getting ingredients for tamales. She'd point to the Vaseline in her cabinet and tell me it was because of her sickness, the diabetes. She needed circulation.

Once, she was on the couch in front of the television watching a *telenovela* and I was rubbing her feet. She dozed off, and I got pissed because I couldn't stop rubbing until she told me to stop. It took a lot of rubbing to get the blood going, she said. So I pressed hard with my thumbs.

In the desk drawer by the telephone she kept needles for injections. *Insulina*, she called it. I went and grabbed one, smaller than a safety pin, and took off the plastic wrapping then held it between my fingers. Tencha's hands were over her stomach and her head was tilted to the side. For a second I thought I should leave her alone. She looked peaceful and hadn't even noticed I wasn't rubbing her anymore.

But the needle was in my hand, so I poked her in the foot.

"¿Qué haces?" she yelled, looking scary and scared at the same time. Her fingers were spread open trying to reach for her foot. I started laughing because she couldn't reach, and I hadn't poked her that hard, just enough for the needle to stick in, like a splinter. *"¡Luz! ¿Qué chingao?"*

I took it out and ran out of the house and climbed the pecan tree that was in the backyard. She came out screaming for what felt like an hour, telling me it hurt. And would I like it if she poked me when I was sleeping? She told me how insensitive I was to take advantage of *una enferma* that couldn't even work today. She had all these tamale orders she had to finish, but she couldn't stand for very long, which meant she couldn't push down with the weight the *masa* needed in order to be done right. If I didn't respect my elders, *Diosito* would punish me! "You better pray hard," she said, asking what was wrong with me. What happened? What's gotten into you? She yelled until she tired herself out, then walked inside. I heard her change the channels on the television before I climbed down and found her sleeping again, snoring with her mouth half-open and her socks and slippers over her feet. She went back to where she was, in some dream, some other place, and I sat across from her as I heard her say, "Insensitive," over and over again. How can you be so insensitive, mama? You're not like that. What's gotten into you? That's not who you are. What's wrong with you? Talk to me, what's going on?

As I watched her sleep all those questions made me feel as if I'd melt right there all over the floor. What's wrong? What's gotten into you? Talk to me, mama.

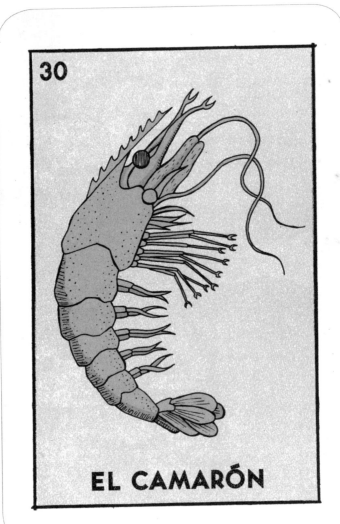

30

EL CAMARÓN

EL CAMARÓN

Papi would get behind Mom when she was cooking and sway from side to side. She'd throw his hands off, and because she wasn't easy he would push her forward and the skillet would clatter.

Then she'd get mad and be gone. Out the door and in her car. Off somewhere.

She used to say, forgive and forget, but I don't think she believed it, because how can you forget about the things you feel?

Papi's *cabezón*. *Muy cabezón*. He'll break you in half,

and I have a dislocated wrist to prove it. When someone notices my wrist, with the bone sticking out and the lump on top, I tell them, "My dad broke it because I jerked off my *primo*." Like that, they know how *cabezón* he is. You'd think I hate him. But it doesn't matter; it doesn't mean I don't love him.

One time Estrella talked back to him and he slapped her so hard she was knocked out for two minutes. When she woke up she ran to her friend Angélica's house down the street with her face all sloppy. And maybe it was too hard, maybe it was too much. But once she was out of the house Papi did to himself what he did to me, like Pedro Infante in *Nosotros los pobres*. I watched him in the kitchen from the hallway and Don Pedro was on the table. I knew he needed some of it so he'd have the guts. I wanted to tell him he didn't have to do it. The movie was just a movie and it wasn't real. But I kept quiet and watched the whole thing, flinching every time he hit his hand against the wall. Once he was done, I went to the freezer and took out a bag of frozen shrimp so he could ice his hand. It was all purple and swollen. I grabbed a kitchen towel and rinsed it with warm water and cleaned the blood from his hand and from the wall. He didn't say or do anything but keep his head down, embarrassed. "*Cabezón*," I said. "*Eres muy cabezón*, Papi."

That night I figured he fought us not because he didn't love us but because he believed in right and wrong. There were right things and wrong things. And when you did a wrong thing, you got a *chingaso*. It wasn't any different when it came to Mom. It wasn't any different when it came to him.

LA GARZA

LA GARZA

It was a morning after Papi had beaten her. He was still asleep in his bedroom and so was Estrella, in ours. I should've been asleep too, but I'd had some dream that woke me up. I opened my eyes and the sunlight was on my face. I went to the kitchen for some water and there was a loaf of bread on the table with a jar of peanut butter next to it. There wasn't any coffee. I grabbed a glass and filled it with water when I noticed the garage door open from the kitchen window. I could see Mom's skinny legs as she was putting something into a suitcase, or some bag.

I thought it'd be nice to go outside and surprise her, sing something. *Estas son las mañanitas* . . . sing a serenade even though it wasn't her birthday. But it was early, so early I saw the sunlight over the kitchen floor. I looked at the clock in the living room. 6:43 a.m. How do I remember? 6:43. I made a pot of coffee because I wanted to go out with a fresh cup, hot, the way she liked. If she were organizing the garage, I'd help her. If she didn't want to talk, I'd be there to make sure she was okay.

I folded a kitchen towel four times and grabbed the coffee cup. It was too hot, and hot enough. I filled it to the top and walked out the door, then three steps down and over to where she was, her back turned to me. She was choosing things from the boxes she opened, and I was about to sing when I saw her putting a photo album in a duffel bag filled with jeans and underwear.

"What are you doing?"

She turned quickly and I noticed the left side of her mouth was swollen. I'd seen parts of her like that before, but I never knew where they'd be. Not until she turned around. I held out the cup and forgot about the box, or suitcase, or duffel bag, and saw only her face. "You want some ice?"

When she realized I was staring at her it was like something changed. She pushed the duffel bag, a bag I'd never seen before, against the wall with her legs and started swallowing and wiping her nose with the back of her hand. I couldn't tell whether she was about to cry or laugh, or both, but she sat there and covered her mouth like if a word was about to come out and she wanted to keep it to herself.

"Where are you going?"

"Nowhere," she said.

I handed her the cup. Even with the kitchen towel underneath, it was burning my hand. "I made you some coffee."

"Is there something you need?" she said, then set the cup down on the ground and covered her mouth.

"No," I said. "Just made you some coffee. But why did you make peanut butter sandwiches?"

"What do you mean?"

"Did you make them for breakfast?"

"Can't I make peanut butter sandwiches?"

"Mom?"

"What?" She stood up and turned around, lifting the duffel bag to the top shelf against the wall.

"You want some ice?"

She said she was reorganizing things. She pushed a box toward me and said, "Here, open this and see what's inside." It was a box filled with clothes from when we were younger.

"What am I looking for?"

"Just clean it! Okay? Can you do that, Luz?"

I shrugged like if I didn't know.

We didn't say anything after that. She drank her coffee little by little, in between stacking boxes on shelves, then pulled out two peanut butter sandwiches from the duffel bag she was filling. She gave one to me and I stopped looking for whatever I was supposed to be looking for. Then, right when I needed something to drink to wash down the peanut butter, I heard Papi at the back door. *"¿Que chingao están haciendo?"*

And I ran inside.

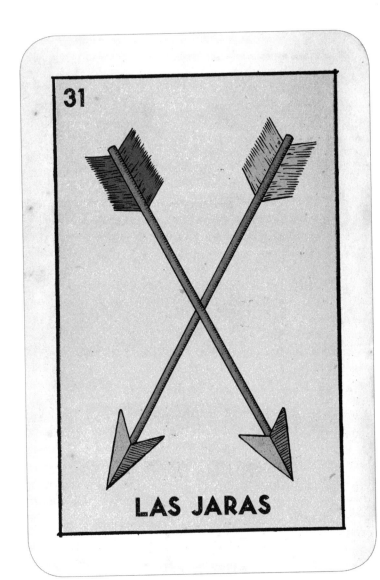

31

LAS JARAS

LAS JARAS

You know that feeling when you fall on your back and the wind is knocked out of you? Or when you're underwater and you can't hold your breath so you swim to the top? Or when you wake up sweating from a dream and can't figure out what's real and what's make-believe? That feeling in your stomach when you're caught doing something you're not supposed to? Or when you discover something for the very first time? That feeling when you got on a roller coaster and you were only eight years old but you felt like a grown-up because finally you got on?

Or when you're in a car and it's going so fast it feels like it's going to flip at any moment? That feeling five minutes before you open your Christmas presents? That feeling like if snakes are inside your stomach and they're trying to get out? Or that feeling after you've hurt someone? When you go over it again and again in your head, what you did and how it happened, how you hit her so hard the bruises proved how bad you were? Even if she didn't bleed you knew she was hurting. Or that feeling when you're on the road and your stomach drops because you drove over a bump? When you're looking at the clouds and out of nowhere it feels like something creeps up on you like a spider? That feeling when you walk up to a convenience store and see someone holding up the register with a gun? You back away and run to the nearest corner, or behind a fence, or a tree, or a mailbox, and wait to see what happens. That feeling when you're holding a gun and it crosses your mind that you can kill someone? This thing in your hand can take someone? It comes and goes like a passing car in the middle of the night and you don't even know where it came from. That feeling when you're underwater and you start to wonder what it would be like if you stayed there and held your breath? You could stay there and deal with the panic and the not knowing whether or not you'll shoot up like an arrow or stay where you are like a stone. That feeling when your body is not even yours anymore? You tell it to stop shaking, but it doesn't. It keeps trembling like if you're in some cold place and you don't even have any clothes to cover yourself with. But it's not the cold. It's something else, something different. And you don't even know where it's coming from.

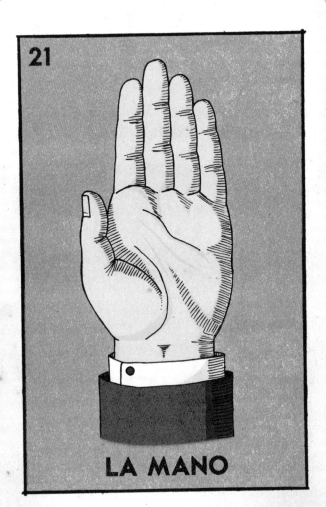

21

LA MANO

LA MANO

My fingernails would get black when we cleaned the house. Papi would do everything that had to do with the yard, and sometimes, in between scrubbing the tub and vacuuming the rooms, I'd go outside and pull the weeds.

Estrella would be in charge of folding underwear on the living room floor, and sometimes I'd help her. She'd sit Indian-style next to a pile of white and pink and blue, and the Bounce Mom would throw in the dryer would make me think it was what clouds smelled like.

Papi's boxers were the easiest. Panties and bras weren't.
I sat with my legs open and sometimes Estrella would sit
on her heels. I tried sitting that way but it was uncomfort-
able. We didn't have the same hips. I had Papi's hips and
she had Mom's. When I tried to lengthen my neck and sit
up taller, because I felt short and round, it didn't look the
same, not like when Estrella sat up.

●   ●   ●

We were washing our hands in the bathroom. Mom was
making dinner and Papi was on the couch watching television. We were washing our hands at the same time over the
sink, but I finished before her and felt I'd done it wrong, so
I washed them again. And still I finished before her. I said,
"Why you taking so long?"

"Because, I'm doing it right."

"Smart-ass," I said, and splashed her face.

We'd decided, between all of us, that *pendeja* wasn't a
maldición but smart-ass was, so she yelled, "Luz called me
a smart-ass!"

But before she could finish the sentence I grabbed her hair and pulled it, trying to make her shut up.

She called Mom but Papi came and pulled us apart. He grabbed me by my hand and took me to his bedroom and closed the door and took off his belt. He opened his hand and looked at me and said, *"¿Lista?"* And I nodded.

He pulled his arm back and lifted his eyebrows and slapped the belt against his hand as hard as he could, and I let out a yelp to make it seem as though he were hitting me.

39

EL NOPAL

EL NOPAL

I didn't feel like remembering today so I laid out the cards close to each other so that they were touching like tiles, like *El Nopal*. Now they make up a collage and the water cards are on the bottom and the sun is on top.

I asked Papi once what the sun riddle meant and he said it was the roof of the poor. *La cobija de los pobres*. To the right of it I put *El Catrin* and to the left *La Dama*. *El Corazón* is at the center, and below it, *El Tambor*. Between them they make music. *El Árbol* is next to them, then *La Rosa* with *La Chalupa* and *La Garza* two cards over. Below is *El Mundo y El Diablito*. Next to them there's the harp. If there were two I'd put one by the star and the other under the rest, where it's at, so that in a way all of them could be close to the sound of music. On the opposite side are the parrot and bird, *los primos*. They fly in and out of the other cards. The Flag, the Soldier, the Indian, the Drunk. *La Sirena* is on the left. I laid them out and she ended up there, not far from the edge. I looked at the frog for a long time because I didn't know where to put her. Her dopey eyes look like she's about to jump. Like if she can see a fly we can't see, and what do they eat, anyway? Those stupid eyes, the way she sits there. Wouldn't it be funny if she jumped? Where would she go?

I went through the deck three times and I can't find *El Gallo*. Maybe *he* jumped? Maybe he sang himself to death and no one heard him and so he went out the door and down the hall and out the building, cawing like he does to wake people up. But no one heard him, and we missed it. Maybe I left him at the house when I came here, which means by now he's been swept up in the trash or hiding under a piece of furniture. If he were here I'd put him by the sun. Maybe he's in some dark place trying to get someone's attention, singing like he does, *"Kikirikiki! Kikirikiki!"*

Estrella had her own card, but there isn't one called *La Luz*, so I chose *El Sol* as my own. But in the way that The Star needs The Moon, Luz needs *El Gallo* and so maybe without him I don't have a voice. So what happens when something is missing? It's like the thing that's missing might be the one thing I need in order to win. And why do I always need the one thing that isn't here?

Why don't You bring her back so she can show them that she hit him too? That it's not his fault. Like that they will let him go.

And how loud do I have to sing before You wake up?

¿Dónde está El Gallo?

45

EL VENADO

EL VENADO

It was only a matter of time before we woke up and found her missing. I don't know what we expected, but we were expecting something. And when it happened I went straight to the kitchen cabinet to see if there was any peanut butter left.

Mom was usually the first to wake up in the mornings, to make a pot of coffee and put the dishes away. The morning she was gone we figured she was getting milk at the grocery store. But it was different. Everything was the same as the night before. The dishes were in the sink and the table hadn't been wiped. Liters of Coke were still on the counter, all warm. It was like she waited for us to fall asleep and then got her suitcase and went wherever she was going.

Papi didn't come out of his room until later, and I wondered what their bedroom looked like. Maybe he realized she was gone because something was missing. Or maybe everything was the same. None of us spoke about it, not until the following day.

It was almost a year ago when she left. I was ten and Estrella was twelve.

• • •

The following morning Papi was in his room and Estrella and I were sitting on the steps that lead to the backyard. She kept asking me if I was okay, like all of a sudden *she* was my mother.

"You know she loves us, right?"

"Yeah, I know," I said. "She'll be back."

"No, mama," she said, and touched my shoulder.

I pulled away from her and said, "Who do you think you're calling mama?"

She snapped and said she wasn't going to try to help me if I was going to be that way. "Help me with what?"

I asked, and pushed her. She pushed me back and then I punched her in the chest and she ran inside. I chased her to the bathroom but she couldn't get the door open and so she lifted her arms in front of her. I kept punching her even though she cried.

"How's that, mama?" I said. "You like that, mama? Huh, mama?"

We were next to Papi's room and he opened the door and screamed, *"¿Qué chingao?"* We backed away and Estrella's hair was all over the place. Her face was puffy and neither of us said anything. The sunlight was coming in from the window on the other side of Papi's bedroom, and it only took a few seconds of us standing there, looking at each other, before I could tell we were thinking about her and wondering whether she was coming back.

Behind him, past his window, I saw something move. I heard Estrella sucking in her saliva, but when I felt something in the backyard, I turned. I couldn't help it. Papi turned and saw it too. A deer was standing next to our only tree, staring at us with his brown marble eyes.

Then he ran off.

34

EL SOLDADO

EL SOLDADO

When she disappeared, Papi didn't eat for weeks. We'd find him holding photographs of her in one hand and a lighter in the other, flicking it on and off, thinking of whether or not to burn her face off. Sometimes he did because we found photos in the family album where there was a burned circle over a woman with a blue dress on. But I never heard him say he wanted to burn her face off. He just didn't want to see her face.

The clothes Mom left behind were there to remind us, because who knew if she was coming back. Papi held the lighter but it wasn't like he didn't miss her, wasn't like he wasn't trying to figure out where she ran off to. Estrella and I thought about where she went, and whenever we'd mention it to him, he'd tell us to shut up.

That's when Estrella started having ideas. She thought maybe they got into a fight and this time it was so bad that something happened. "But why would he burn her face off?" I said. "He wouldn't do that unless she hurt him too."

Why would he want to forget her? He burned her face, but then he held her photograph. Even though he didn't want us talking about her, I saw him holding it, flicking the lighter on and off. And maybe it was because she said something or did something. She told him she was leaving and he hit her. But what about us? Why would she leave? She could've come to us in the middle of the night and whispered, "Get in the car! Come on." Maybe I would've said no. Maybe Estrella would've said yes.

• • •

A few weeks after Mom was gone, it was a Sunday and Papi was still sleeping and we tried to make noise in the kitchen. Estrella washed the dishes while I opened and closed cabinets. When he came out of his bedroom he didn't even notice we were standing there. We could've been monkeys and it wouldn't have mattered. We asked him if he wanted some eggs.

I was putting the dishes away and put the bowls on the wrong shelf. Estrella said I wasn't putting them where they belong. Mom would never put them there. Then he snapped, *"¡Cállense!"* and went back to his room.

• • •

Before Papi had a chance to throw everything away, Estrella and I took some of Mom's stuff and hid it in our room under our beds. Most of it clothes. Only one suitcase was missing from the garage and we figured she had packed as much as she could. No photos, no knickknacks, not even all her shoes. Just whatever she could pack into one suitcase.

There was a T-shirt she used to wear to go to bed, baby blue cotton. Estrella brought it into our room, and I was shocked she hadn't taken it. I thought it was something she'd want. It was too big for me, but I put it on and liked the way it felt against my skin. Estrella and I would take turns wearing it, but we were afraid the smell would disappear if we wore it for too long.

Estrella was at Angélica's house when Papi caught me in my room wearing it. It wasn't a school day. I remember sunlight coming in and Papi looking tanned against it, standing at the doorway with his boxers on. He had a mustache. He'd grown one after Mom had left, and on that day, it looked real pokey, like a scrub.

"*¿Y eso?*" he asked. He scared me, because I didn't see him standing there. Mom's T-shirt would blow up around my hips if I spun around, and so I was spinning and humming a song. His arm was against the wall and his armpit was black.

"Answer me," he said.

I figured he wanted me to take it off and burn it or something. His feet came closer, so close I could smell him. He smelled like an unmade bed. "*Dámelo,*" he said, and his voice hit the top of my head. But I didn't move, and I wasn't going to give it to him.

"*Dame,*" he said, then hit me like if I didn't hear him. I lifted my arms. After he pulled it off, I felt naked underneath. I saw him smelling it. "What are you going to do with it?" I asked. But he didn't say anything.

I stood there in the middle of the room staring at the carpet with my fingers hooked in front of me.

"*Oye,*" he said, and I looked up. "What?" I said.

"*No dices* 'what,' " he said.

"*¿Mande?*" I said.

"*¿Mande,* what?"

"*¿Mande, Papi?*"

I was wearing nothing but panties and I was already ten. But all I could think of was how much I wanted him to understand what I was feeling. I lifted my head and stood there as strong as I could because I wanted him to know that even though he missed the way she smelled, the way she was, the way she looked, he was taking her from me. I stared at him in the eyes and the light in the room was all gold and I didn't have a shirt on and my hair was all *pelos parados*. I tried my hardest to show him how I felt with my eyes. And maybe. Maybe You passed through me. Maybe You spoke in a way my voice couldn't, because then, it was like he saw something in the way I was looking at him, and he threw it back to me, in a gentle kind of way and it landed over my face.

46

EL SOL

EL SOL

It was ripe outside and we were lying out on the grass. Estrella was wearing the white bikini Papi bought her at Target, and I was wearing Hanes with small yellow fish. Papi was wearing boxers, the ones with blue stripes, rolled down two times.

"You're going to burn if you do that," I said, but Estrella looked at her skin like if she were made of something expensive. She'd brought a container of Crisco outside and was smoothing it over her legs. Her nails had been painted red the night before and she was wearing black sunglasses. "The bees are going to get us. We're going to have to go inside."

"*Mija*, let her be," Papi said, as he sprayed us with the garden hose in his hand. The water was cold but it felt good in the heat, and I stuck out my tongue.

Estrella picked up her towel, lay down farther away from us, and started mumbling, "Ugh, Ugh . . . UGH!" Like if it were some language me and Papi were supposed to understand. "Be that way then," I said. "I hope you burn."

She looked at the sun with her sunglasses on and propped herself up on her elbows. Papi lay down, wiggling his toes as if ants were on him, and I lay down next to him. After five minutes I turned on my stomach and could hear a bee flying close to my shoulder. I saw Estrella lift the string of her bikini to see if she'd gotten any color.

"Take it off," Papi said. And I thought the same. If she didn't want any tan lines, she should just take it off.

"I'm not taking it off!" she said.

"*¿Y por qué no?* You want a tan so bad. Just take it off," he said. He'd been drinking since breakfast. "No one's going to look at you."

I turned around and saw him taking off his boxers. He took them off, like normal, and tossed them behind him, laughing. I'd never seen him naked before. "That's why we have fences," he said, then plopped down on his stomach with his *pompis* in the air.

"Yeah," I said. "No one's going to see you. No one cares, don't be stupid." She was so disgusted she got up and went inside.

Papi turned and looked at me and made a face like, Oh well. He shut his eyes from the glare of the sun and said, *"Ándale, ¡otra!"* Like when I'd dance for him by the garage. Or when he'd play music on the boom box. Or when he'd want another beer.

"¡Otra!"

I closed my eyes and fell asleep, and because there wasn't Crisco in the air, there wasn't a single bee that came near us.

52

LA MACETA

LA MACETA

"¡Cállate, chingada madre!"

Tencha would get mad sometimes and change colors, sometimes yellow, sometimes green. But when she was in a good mood she'd put on her one-piece and swim with me in the pool. She'd say, *"Somos sirenas."* All cute. Then wiggle her hips and call me *sirenita*.

I'd stay underwater in her pool for as long as I could and she'd think I was drowning. I could stay there for so long that if she saw me she'd think I was dying. I'd come out and see her at the edge of the pool getting close to me, all red, all over, moving like a gorilla. Like when they look confused. Yelling, *"¿Qué haces? ¡Estás loca!"*

"No," I'd tell her. But she couldn't hear me because her voice was louder than mine. I'd keep saying it as she dragged me toward the table under the portico. She'd dig her thumbs into my cheeks and pull down like if she wanted to see what was behind my eyes. *"¡Me asustaste!"* she'd say. Then I felt bad because her breath would shorten. Like if she couldn't breathe. She'd rub her heart and say things like, "And what do I tell your Papi if something happened? What do I tell the police? How can you be so stupid?" She'd say so many things I wouldn't have time to say anything back. And when she calmed herself down she'd give me a spoonful of sugar, pull me to her chest, and hold me so hard I could hardly breathe.

• • •

I walked into her house one day and saw Estrella telling Tencha that Papi was hitting her. Tencha was holding her arm like if she was about to tear it off, telling her she shouldn't say *maldiciones*. Papi was a good, good man and he'd never do anything to hurt her. How in the hell could those words come out of her mouth? Tencha let go of Estrella's arm when she saw me and called out my name like if she had forgotten who I was, but then remembered.

Estrella wasn't supposed to say anything. "What did you say?" I said. And she got all attitude like she does. Because she's older. Tencha looked at her and started screaming, saying she was a *malcriada*, to say *maldiciones*, to disrespect her father like that. Estrella looked at me and shook her head No, No, No. Because she knew I was lying and she was telling the truth. But I pointed to her like if she were some dirty rag a dog would lick. "He doesn't hit you unless you deserve it!" I said.

Tencha grabbed a flowerpot and slammed it down on the floor. She screamed, *"¡Cállense ya, chingada madre!"*

We looked at her and the dirt on the floor. And because she'd said *madre*, not on purpose, I thought of Mom. Estrella thought of her too because her eyes welled up like if the words themselves had hit her across the face, and that's when I knew why she was saying things about Papi. Tencha told her to go home and to lock herself in her room and pray until she knew what she'd said was wrong. Papi wouldn't hit us unless he had to. There was a right way and a wrong way. Papi did things the right way. And when it was time to protect us, he would. "You think he's not allowed to hit you?" she said. "Huh? You don't know what it's like to be beaten! You better be grateful you don't have your Buelo Fermín looking after you." Then she called Estrella *¡Una chiflada! Una desgraciada!*

Estrella ran out of the house and Tencha mumbled something under her breath. *"Que Dios la bendiga."* Then she looked at me in surprise like if she'd forgotten I was standing there. I ran to the pool and held my breath and jumped inside.

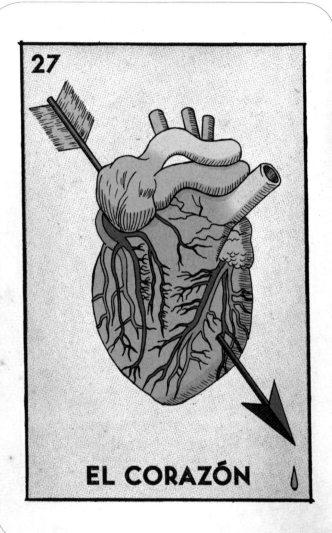

EL CORAZÓN

EL CORAZÓN

When Tencha told me about it later she cried like if she were lost. She was at a friend's house when she got the phone call and didn't know what was going on until she drove down our street and saw the neighbors standing in our yard. The red lights, the white and blue. The crowd of neighbors. The police officers and yellow tape pulled around the trees.

She wanted to know what had happened, the way she was looking at me sitting in a room at the police station, upset that I wouldn't say anything. But I couldn't get any sound out. The officers told her what happened, but she wanted to hear it from me. I could tell she wanted to hit me like if I were a broken machine, but she didn't. She kept squeezing her nose and wiping her eyes. She held me and then let go, held me again, like if she were confused of what to do. She couldn't decide whether to stay with me or go to the hospital to see Estrella.

Eventually, she left because it was time for visitors to leave, and that thing started, when it's hard for her to breathe. "I'll come in the morning," she said. But it's like she's too big for her own breath and she chokes on the things she tries to say.

In that room, not this one but the other one before here, the pillow was flat and hard like sand and I had to act like I was asleep before they turned off the light. I was alone with just a window and it was me and the sound of my heart, and my body, and the beat of it.

Sometimes, even now, it's like someone is knocking on the door of my chest and I'm on the other side trying to figure out how to open it. But it won't open, and so it bangs and bangs. *Poom! Poom! Poom!*

Until my mind shuts off and I fall asleep.

EL PÁJARO

EL PÁJARO

Remember the yellow birds that used to sing pretty? We'd run in circles in Buelita Fe's backyard after church and they'd come and they'd sing and we'd dance. There were two of them. We'd call them Hector and Louise. I looked up at the cloud above the garage and You told me. You said, "This is Hector. This is Louise." Then I flapped my arms and ran on my toes and got all excited like I was going to explode *¡pee pee pee pee pee!* For a long time I didn't know they were yellow. I never saw them just heard them. They were sounds coming from the tomatillo vines. You told me to look up when they were singing instead of when they were quiet because when they were quiet they were flying around the house. And when they were singing they were sitting in the tree. There was one time Hector landed on the edge of the fountain. He looked at me, then at the barbecue grill, then at You. And flew away. I ran after him but got as far as the fence. He wasn't in the tree anymore and neither was Louise. And every Sunday after that it was quiet.

18

EL VIOLONCELLO

EL VIOLONCELLO

Tencha came to tell me he was here. Dr. Roberto. "He's in the activity room waiting for you."

"What does he want?" I said.

"He wants to give you something."

There are tables along the windows with game boards stacked on top, Checkers, Scrabble, Monopoly. He was sitting at the far end with a white button-up shirt and the light coming in through the blinds drew bars over his face. He held his hands over the table.

"Just let him give you whatever he wants to give you,"

she said, and pushed me toward him. "Then he'll leave you alone."

She stood in the hallway and monitored me as I walked toward him. He saw me and sat up straight in his chair. The way dogs do when they see you coming. No one else was in the room. The other kids in the center were down the hall playing with blocks, squealing, knocking towers over. Julia was sitting in the counselor's office across the hall. I sat down and looked at his hands, then looked out the window. After a few minutes he reached into his bag and took out a book from his briefcase. Hans Christian Andersen, it said, in big blue letters across the top.

"Your mom always said you like to read." He turned the book around and pushed it toward me. There was a boy in a boat on the cover, all alone in the middle of the sea. "I thought you might like this," he said.

We sat there without saying anything. I looked across the hall and saw Julia looking up from her desk. When she saw me, she turned away.

This redhead boy who's been at the center for two days started crying in the other room. I recognized his voice because his screams remind me of a siren. A counselor walked out with him in her arms and took him outside, bouncing him up and down, patting his head. I could see them through the window. I stared at his face, the way it looked as if it were being torn.

"How's your hand?" Dr. Roberto said.

I rolled my eyes, wanting him to leave me alone, wanting to go back to my room.

"You like to read?" he asked.

Yeah, you stupid. I like to read. I looked at him, and he mentioned that he should've gotten me something else, something more grown-up, since I wasn't a child anymore.

He took a long, deep breath and held his hands like if he were washing them. "I wanted to tell you how sorry I am," he said.

Then I looked at him in that sort of way I do when I try to tell people I hate them. I pushed the table as hard as I could and the edge of it slammed into his chest. The book fell on the floor and I ran to my room and closed the door and Tencha called after me, "Luz! What'd he say to you?" She knocked on the door. *"¿Luz? ¿Qué pasó?"*

From the window in my room I saw him get into his car. He opened the door and stood there with his arms over the roof. He stared at the building like if he couldn't decide if he wanted to leave or not. But in my head, I thought, *Leave. Leave, you asshole. Go already*. Then he got into his car and drove away. When he was out of the parking lot I was mad I hadn't asked him. But I couldn't when he was in front of me. If I could've I would have: "Where is she?"

"Luz? *Mija*, let me in."

Tencha knocked on the door as I lay in bed. I looked at the ceiling with my journal in my arms. I could hear that redhead boy from down the hall screaming and I tried to turn his siren into music, into a note, like a string. But she kept knocking. And after a few minutes, she knocked again.

8

LA BOTELLA

LA BOTELLA

When he wasn't looking, I used to look at the label and see if there was a face on it like Papi's. There were those nights when his eyes would get bloodshot and I'd want to drink with him. Not a lot, just a sip, so I could see what it was like to become him. To be someone else and to knock things over without caring. I didn't want to hit or hurt anyone. I just wanted to know where it came from, to figure out why he did what he did because it wasn't coming from him. It was coming from that man in the bottle, Don Pedro. He'd get inside

Papi's head and shake him until he turned into someone else. Like if he were in some storm and the wind that blew threatened him off balance if he fought back. But Papi *did* fight back and he held on to the boat that was his body as it spun and crashed, because that's how he moved, like if he were on a boat in the middle of an ocean. And when he'd lose his grip he'd lose his balance and step over his feet, then hold on to something else and try to fight again, looking up at the sky and yelling in its face, *"¡Estás loca! ¿Me oyes? ¡Loca!"*

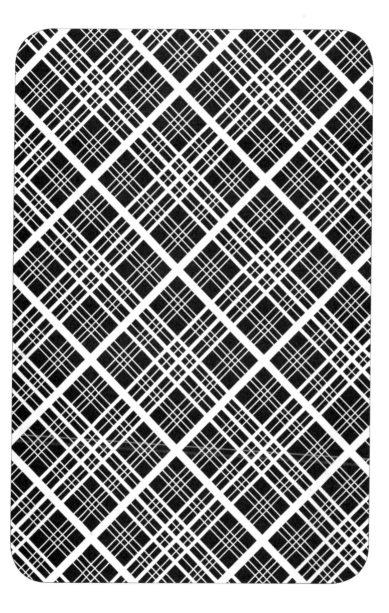

EL ÁRBOL

EL ÁRBOL

When they used to fight I'd grab a knife from the kitchen counter and stab the tree in the backyard. Estrella would go to Angélica's. Sometimes she would even go to Tencha's, and minutes later, there'd be a knock on the door. Mom would go to the bedroom and Papi would answer. *"¿Qué quieres?"* No hello. No nothing. Just, "What do you want?"

"Wanted to visit," Tencha'd say, and get inside and have coffee and talk about Buelito Fermín in Reynosa. He was feeling better since he started his new medication. But

Papi never seemed to care and sometimes he'd even say it was time for that *viejo* to rest in peace. I'd walk around the house and look into Mom's bedroom from the windows, but her blinds were usually pulled down. Sometimes she'd come out with a towel wrapped around her head, and wearing a bathrobe. Her body red from a hot shower and smelling like Flex shampoo. But if something was sore, she'd stay in her bedroom until Tencha left. Then Papi would leave too, taking the bottle with him.

Two days later Mom would make almond cookies and walk to Tencha's. She'd talk about everything but the bruises, and sometimes I'd go with her and sit there, not saying anything, waiting for her to say something. But it was like a topic that wasn't supposed to be talked about, and that's how I learned not to say anything. Tencha would look at me and caress my cheek, like if by touching it she'd protect it from getting hurt.

• • •

After Mom was gone, there was no reason to keep stabbing the tree, but the marks stayed. I'd pass the tree and see the skin get darker. I'd feel the splinters and the grooves like if they were wounds.

One time Estrella called Papi *un hijo de puta* the way Mom used to do and he slapped her so hard he split her lip with one of his rings. She called him an asshole because he wouldn't tell us where Mom was or what had happened, and she believed he knew.

She said he was lying.

49

EL PINO

EL PINO

T he truck is a piece a shit," Papi said. He'd bought it from someone he worked with. I liked it because it had a handle for the window to go up and down instead of a button. So the window was going up and down, up and down, and Rocío Durcal was on the radio, a cassette we listened to all the time of a live performance in Acapulco. It was Sunday, early morning, and while most people were heading to mass we were going to buy a tree. Just the two of us. It was going to be the first Christmas without Mom. It had been awhile since she'd disappeared and it seemed okay to talk about her.

"Papi."

"*¿Qué?*"

"Where do you think she went?"

He looked out the window, cranked the volume up, and pushed down on the accelerator. We were the only ones on the highway. Nothing but billboards of whiskey and Denny's. Rocío was singing a duet with Juan Gabriel. I rolled the window up and crossed my arms and waited.

"She went to Mexico and she's coming back when she's ready. That's what I think," I said, as loud as I could, as loud as Rocío was singing. But he didn't say anything.

I looked out the window even though I wanted to tell him what he needed to hear. That he was a drunk, and he'd turn into someone else because he didn't like her working for Dr. Roberto. The way she used to get dressed before going to work for him. And it wasn't his fault. It was Don Pedro. When he'd drink, Estrella and I would go to our rooms or go to Tencha's because we didn't know who he'd turn into. He needed to snap out of it. Like in that movie when the actress slaps the guy's face and says, "Snap out of it!" That's what I wanted to say to him and that's what I wanted to do.

"Papi?" He looked straight ahead and then at me.

"Snap out of it!" I said.

He veered off the highway onto the feeder, and nothing but tall pines were around us. Gray clouds and an empty road. He stopped at a red light and it turned green but he didn't move. There were no cars in front or behind us. His eyes were full of water like after a yawn and he opened his arms and motioned to give him a hug. I unbuckled the seatbelt and leaned over and he squeezed me so hard I didn't know what to do with all the strength he used, holding me like that.

I reminded him that we were at a traffic light and we had to keep going. The light had turned green. We drove on and didn't say anything until we got to the nursery. But by then already the air felt easier.

There were rows of trees right where we parked. The tree we both wanted was right in front of us. I joked that we could get cheeseburgers a lot faster if we got this one, and without answering, Papi went to the man and bought it.

We got back in the truck and rewound the cassette tape to the beginning and sang loud, most of the time off-key because neither of us have a voice like Rocío. We sang every song until it came to "Amor eterno," the song Juan Gabriel wrote about when his mom died. We couldn't go past the first line. Papi looked down at the side-view mirror, at the pine branches sticking out from behind the truck, and every time Rocío raised her voice, singing and screaming at the same time, it felt like if the front seats were flooding with water.

35

LA ESTRELLA

LA ESTRELLA

They were out when they came to get Papi. I remember the officers holding me down outside even
though I wasn't struggling. I could see the stars at the top
of the sky and hear Papi yelling as they pushed him inside
the car. And the sirens were loud, though far. Estrella was
being rushed to the hospital and everyone around me kept
saying, "Stop moving! Stop moving!"

Was I moving?

Papi was in the kitchen when the officers knocked on
the door. I was in the bathroom. We were frying chicken

for dinner and later when it'd burn I wouldn't know if the smell was the burning or something else. They asked Papi if he was José Antonio Castillo, and after he said yes, they asked about Mom, Cristina María Castillo. Before they could finish saying her name, Papi raised his voice and said she'd run off already a year now. They wanted him to go down to the station for questioning and that's when I heard the door close. I thought that was the end of it, that they'd leave us alone. But they banged on the door and said, "Mr. Castillo, open the door!" They yelled. "Open the door!" He'd been drinking, and I knew from the sound of the banging that it'd set something off inside of him. The door opened, and the yelling got louder. They must've noticed he'd been drinking because of the way he stumbled. They tried to handcuff him, saying things like he was under arrest for assaulting an officer and for the suspected murder of Cristina María Castillo. When I heard those words, I peeked from the hallway and looked for her because I knew it was Estrella who'd gone and told them. She'd run away two days before and Papi kept telling me she'd be back. "She'll be back, *mija*. Don't worry.

You'll see." The front door was left open and down the sidewalk was another officer standing behind her with his hands on her shoulders, like if she were standing in front of school and it was her first day.

I saw Papi in the living room trying to break free from their grip. There were two of them. A white man and a Mexican. The Mexican was speaking Spanish like if Papi didn't understand English, trying to pin him down. I ran to Papi's bedroom and stuck my hand under the mattress and grabbed the rifle. I held it against my chest. "You're under arrest," I heard them say. I walked down the hallway with the rifle aimed toward their voices. The white man must've seen me because I heard him say I had a gun. He backed away with his hands facing me, like if I weren't real and he couldn't believe I'd appeared. He fell to his knees and said, "Put the gun down, little girl. Put it down."

He turned to Papi and asked, "What's her name? Tell her to put it down."

Papi looked at me, and I knew by the way he looked at me he wanted me to do whatever I had to do.

Estrella thought Papi had taken Mom somewhere in the woods and beaten her until she couldn't breathe. She thought he had strangled her. "That's why we can't find her," she said to me. "Because he buried her! He's an animal, Luz! Don't you get it?"

Papi fought back and so they thought he was guilty. That's how it happens. That's why they were in shock when they saw me. They never thought it would come from me. They didn't know I was in the other room.

"Leave him alone!" I shouted.

When they looked at me, stupid and stunned, Papi broke free from their grip and grabbed a knife off the kitchen counter. He saw me and wanted a weapon of his own. He waved it in the air. But he was drunk. He'd been drinking and he lost his balance. Then, behind the officers and through the front door, I saw Estrella running toward the house. The Mexican officer tried to grab the knife and the white officer came toward me. Estrella ran inside, waving her arms, screaming, "DON'T! DON'T!"

But my finger felt stuck around the trigger and the officer grabbed the barrel and I pulled, and he pulled, and then the sound was so loud it knocked me down. On my back, in that moment when the air was knocked out of me, I thought, *It's done. It's over.* They wouldn't take Papi and everything was okay. They just had to leave us alone.

But when I lifted my head I saw her on the ground with her cheek on the floor and her hair over her face. My mouth opened but no sound came out. Other officers came in and grabbed me and carried me out of the house by my arms and legs. Papi screamed like a dog being held down, yelling over and over again, *"¡Hija! ¡Es mi hija!"*

I heard the ambulance. The sirens. But it felt like I was hearing them from underwater. Like if I were sinking and something was filling my ears, and the sounds were beginning to fade, except for Papi screaming.

As they carried me to the car, facing up, all I can remember, all I could see were the stars.

43

LA CAMPANA

LA CAMPANA

We'd go to Buelita Fe's house and hear church bells. *Do—ong! Do—ong! Do—ong!* Go to mass by ten and be out by half past eleven, then be in her backyard playing by the time it struck noon. We'd chase each other and I'd trip on a rock and brush off the dirt from my knees and see the blue and red mix together. I'd get up and run around the tree, go inside the garage and hear it again: *Do—ong! Do—ong!* Not able to find her, I'd stop trying and go inside and forget. When it was over, I could still hear them. She'd creep up and say, "Where'd you go?"

And I'd say, "I'm right here. I've been here the whole time. You're the one who got lost." She'd run inside or to the back of the house and leave me there, sitting by myself, with the bells in my head and the bells in the trees. Still ringing. *Do—ong! Do—ong! Do—ong!*

28

LA SANDÍA

LA SANDÍA

I woke up this morning and I couldn't find my journal. No one was awake so I went to the counselor's office, and there it was on her desk, by the printer next to the phone. I grabbed it and flipped through it. They hadn't changed anything or marked in it, but still. *How did they find it?* It was there. Someone went to my room and took it. And I'm sure they read it, but which part? In the hallway I looked to the exit where the security officer was sitting, leaning back, listening to some news channel on his stupid radio. I went over to him and knocked on the glass, "Hey!" I screamed, and he was shocked by the sound of my voice. It was the first time he had heard it. He flinched and turned around. "What about my rights?" I screamed. They were thieves. The man, tall now, standing, looked at me. "Why aren't you in bed?" "Because!" I yelled. "You like it when people take your things?" "Calm down," he said and opened the door. He tried to reach for my shoulders but I backed away. The hall lights turned on and I heard Larry from down the hall. "What's going on?" he said, coming out of the counselors' lounge. "What?" I said. He looked at the journal in my hand, with his stunned and stupid face, probably because it was the first time he heard my voice. "You took it!" I screamed. "You can't take my things!" Then he tried to catch me, but I kicked him between his legs.

In my room, crying all stupid, my mouth wet, I shoved my bed in front of the door. I went to the shower and turned the cold knob as far as it'd go. The journal got wet when I opened the first page and the letters began to smear. I was about to tear it into pieces so that no one could ever figure out what I'd written. But something stopped me.

I threw it out and it landed on the sink. Then, under the shower, I turned the knob to hot and grabbed it with both hands. I wanted to hit my head against the wall but I was too chicken, then I was mad for being too chicken. My skin turned pink, and to keep moving I grabbed the shampoo and covered myself with it.

Larry and the officer banged on the door, over and over again, until I screamed as loud as I could. "THIEVES! You hear me! THIEVES!"

And then they stopped.

37

EL MUNDO

EL MUNDO

There was a photograph from their wedding day in a frame under the television. You can tell it was Papi who took the shot, the way Mom is running away from him, looking back, the veil between her and the lens. When you look at the photo you know he's smiling too. You can sense it. *Entre ellos no hay nada en el mundo que no tenga sentido.*

Tencha gave me a photo of myself the other day and I tried to remember being a two-year-old sitting on the counter with flour on my face. My hair was red then, which is weird because now it's black. The ones who love me say, *Sí, mija, eres tú.* I have no choice but to believe them. In the photograph, the girl has a smile over her face, her mouth is half-open, and there's a pasty white mess between her fingers.

26

EL NEGRITO

EL NEGRITO

This is what Julia said to me this morning.

"Larry thought it might be a good idea if I was the one who spoke to you. I know it's been awhile since you've been here and that's what I'd like to talk to you about."

I was sitting by the window with hot chocolate in front of me steaming out of a cup.

"I want to apologize," she said. "We're sorry, everyone is very sorry about your notebook. It was very inconsiderate of us and we should've asked your permission. We had no right, but I want you to know, Luz, we thought your notebook would help your father. But—"

Silencio.

She didn't have the balls to explain how wrong she was.

"We'll never take it again. I promise. It's yours, and we're deeply sorry.

"I want to speak to you like a grown-up because I think of you that way, Luz. The way you've coped has been more mature than some of the teenagers here. You're a big girl, and we want you to be protected. Do you understand? It's important for us to provide a good home for you."

I know she wanted me to look at her or respond, but I didn't. I looked down and cleaned the dirt from under my nails.

"Luz, your father has pleaded guilty to aggravated assault of a police officer. The D.A. decided there wasn't enough evidence to charge him with anything else. And that's good news, Luz. He might, or rather, he could get out of prison in three years and live with you again. You can visit him whenever you want if you stay."

Silencio.

"Because there is no legal guardian who can take custody of you, and you *are* an American citizen, we would like to transfer you to *Casa de Esperanza*. We know your

Aunt Tencha has been trying to get her residence permit, but . . . we have to find you a home. You need someone who's going to look after you and take care of you. Luz, you can't live with your aunt here in the United States. She doesn't have a resident permit, and we've been told by immigration that she's never applied for one. She mentioned you might want to go back to Mexico. Is that true? Would you want to go back to Mexico? If you don't want to live at *Casa de Esperanza*, we have decided, for your well-being, to give you the option to return to Mexico with your aunt. But only if you want to. I'm sure your grandfather would love to see you. And you could come back whenever you want and visit your father."

Más silencio.

"Do you understand, Luz? If you want to go visit *Casa de Esperanza*, we can arrange that for you. We're here to help. You know that, right? Do you understand? Do you have any questions?"

The hot chocolate steamed even after she was done talking. Not until it was cold did she get up and leave me alone.

50

EL PESCADO

EL PESCADO

I dreamt of *Angelitos negros* last night. The movie about the mom who has a black baby girl and hates her because she's black. Not until the end of the movie does she find out her "real" mom is the black maid she's had all her life. But in the movie the girl is not even black. They paint her skin with dark makeup and it's obvious she's white. There's a moment in the movie the girl covers herself in flour, and they ask her, "What are you doing?" She says, "I want my mother to love me." And she makes this pouty expression like Shirley Temple. In my dream I was the actress playing the girl, but I was late for work. I didn't have time to put the makeup on, so only half of my face was dark and the other light. I didn't want to get fired, so I ran to the set where we were filming and did the scene anyway. The director said something looked different. Something was off. "No, no, nothing's off," I said. "I think you forgot, you said we'd be shooting underwater today. So maybe that's what it is." He said, "Oh yeah, let's move it!" We all packed our things, lights, costumes. Pedro Infante and I talked about where we were going for lunch, hoping this one taco vendor was going to be near the parking lot in his usual spot during break. Then, all of a sudden, we were all underwater and I couldn't hear at first, let alone see, but we moved through the scene as if it were normal, like if we'd done it before. And down there, the makeup came off anyway, so it didn't matter. I told the director, "This is so much better, it makes so much more sense," with bubbles around my face. And he tried to tell me something too, so I leaned in closer to him, but I was talking and he was talking and there were bubbles everywhere. I felt his fingers on my lips like if he were trying to tell me to shut up and listen, but his fingers were thin. And slowly, the bubbles floated away and right in front of me was Mom. She was looking at me, holding my shoulders in place, keeping me still and staring at me like if I were in a fishbowl. There was a white light coming off of her and I started to feel happy, without saying anything at all, just feeling happy because she was giving me tips in a movie I was in, directing me here and there, saying don't cry so much in this part, don't move around so much when people say their lines. I nodded at everything she said because I understood, and I wanted to make her happy. I wanted to make her proud. As I looked at her, all quiet, all still, I saw the dark blue fingerprints around her neck, like two hands wrapped around her throat that had become stained on her skin. And when she saw me looking at them she grabbed my chin and lifted it, then pointed with two fingers to her eyes. Like if to say, "Look here, look up here." And then we floated to the surface as she slowly disappeared.

16

LA BANDERA

LA BANDERA

I wrote most of the cards at the center. Now I'm writing *La Bandera* from a different room. I have three cards left, and I don't know how it's helped, but somehow I want to finish. Maybe this was a way for You to listen, which is really like listening to myself. A way for me to go to communion. I have to believe that if I keep playing it will be for something.

After Julia talked to me two days ago, I went to my room and packed my things and went to the office and said, "Julia."

She was at her desk with her head in her hands.

"Call my aunt," I said. "I want to go home."

• • •

I'd talked with Tencha and tried to convince her that it would only be for a little while, then we could come back once she got her papers. If we could go, then let's go. What are we waiting for? She looked at me and swayed, yes, no, yes, no, then said we could go down and stay with Buelo Fermín if that's what I wanted.

The day we left you'd never know I was there for three weeks. In and out the days went, with those runny eggs in the morning and the television shows, and the other kids screaming. I didn't leave anything for them to remember me by.

Sometimes I wonder if they told Tencha what they read in my journal. I don't think they did because I would've been able to see it on her face. Or maybe I wouldn't.

She always said to me, "There's nothing illegal about him. *Es un buen padre.*"

And I know he is, but what about me? Am I a good daughter?

Most of the time she was asking questions, "You writing? Did you write something like I told you to?" But she never asked what, not since they took it. Maybe if she'd read it she'd say, "No, No, No, that's not true." But that's what we do, right? We tell our own stories. We have our own *tablas*.

We were out of the center and I didn't look back, not even at my desk or that stupid chair. That stupid desk where I built houses of cards and blew them down.

We'd been in the car for about three hours and I started to feel lighter, like if there was wind beneath us. The escort officer stayed far enough behind so that it didn't feel like we were on a leash.

"You know what's missing?" I said.

"*¿Qué?* Missing with what?" Tencha said. She was sweating like a glass of cold water. The window was down and the day was all dusty orange. "In *Lotería*," I said. "You know what should be part of the deck?"

"What?"

"An eagle. How do you say eagle in Spanish?"

"Águila."

"Like Tony Aguilar."

"Yeah, but without the 'r.' "

"Instead of the first card being *El Gallo* it should be an American bird, not a Mexican. Because you can't count on roosters."

"Mama, what are you talking about?"

"Eagles can fly, Tencha. The only thing *gallos* do is scream loud and fight."

We drove farther away from the city and the land became less and less of anything. There were small towns we drove through with posters of Mexican Duvalín outside the stores we passed. But I didn't see anyone walking on the sidewalks or playing in the parks. It was like they knew we were coming and hid inside to avoid being seen.

"When do the hills start coming?" I asked. "When do we go up and down?"

"Not until after the border," she said. "When we get to Mexico."

"I'm not going to have problems, am I? Like you in the States."

"No, mama. You're Mexican," she said. "They're not going to say anything. You can stay for as long as you want. And you can come back whenever you want. Don't worry. I have your birth certificate."

"But I was born here," I said. And she didn't say anything.

We stopped at a small convenience store and bought two Cokes and some *chicharrones*. The lady behind the register spoke to me in Spanish, and I looked at Tencha like if I didn't understand. "You better start practicing," she said. "No one's going to speak to you in English."

In the car, the road rippled and warped like if it were melting. We had to stop at a checkpoint, a place on the road where cars were waiting for an officer to let them pass. It moved forward every two minutes, so it seemed fine, but I felt sick to my stomach. Tencha turned the radio off so she could concentrate, even though she kept saying it was all going to be simple and fine and there was nothing to worry about. We stopped and I could see the officers open the trunk of a car in front of us. They talked to each other for a long time, then called someone on their walkie-talkie.

I looked out the window and saw something in the desert. At first it looked like a black trash bag blowing between the bushes. But I had to squint because whatever it was, it fell over and got up again, then kicked the dirt. "Look! Can you see that?" I said. Tencha looked out and squinted. "*¿Qué?*" she mumbled. Before I answered, I squinted again and tried to focus. If it weren't for when it opened its arms and took two steps, like if he were carrying a crucifix, maybe I wouldn't have said anything.

"There's a man out there!"

"I don't see anything," she said. "You're imagining it."

I looked at her in that way she knew I was serious, but then, when I turned to him, he was gone. "He was there,"

I said, pointing. "He must've fallen, but he was right there, I saw him." She rubbed my thigh and said it was the heat. "Take a nap, mama. You're tired. It's the sun. Close your eyes." I kept looking for him but I couldn't find him. I knew I'd seen him, and so I opened the passenger door and stepped outside.

"Luz! Get in here," she said, looking forward and back like if someone were coming. But I wanted to see him again, with his arms out to You. How could I not think of Papi at the sight of that man trying to walk? I was running away and trying to forget what had happened, but what if I couldn't? What if I couldn't forgive myself? I thought of Papi and how he made me, and how Mom made me, and how their blood is more mine than Tencha's.

One of the cars in front of us made a U-turn and headed back from where we came from. The escort officer behind us turned his head to see it pass. I looked at the road we'd come from, the way it melted into itself from the heat, then looked at Tencha.

"What, mama?" she said.

I didn't say anything because I didn't have to. She knows me. *Somos iguales.*

"What are you thinking in that little head of yours?" she said, with a face that knew me more than I knew myself. Like if it wasn't Tencha looking at me, but You.

I turned my head to the officer in front of us searching the trunk of someone's car. Then to the car driving away behind us.

"What, mama?" she said. "What?"

I knew she might hate me and it'd be a long time before I saw her again. But it was either Mexico or the House of Hope. Maybe I was supposed to run away and open my arms and run through the desert like that man, looking up at You. The way Papi might be doing in his cell, not forgetting but trying to move forward. *Trying* to forgive himself. And maybe if I ran with my arms out You could take me and decide what to do with me. I looked at Tencha in that way you know us Mexicans know how, in the way You taught us. In that way that says I love you so much it hurts. So when I saw her looking at me like if she were seeing a ghost, I grabbed my backpack from the front seat and ran toward the officer behind us, waving my arms above my head and yelling as loud as I could, *"KIKIRIKIKI!! KIKIRIKIKI!! KIKIRIKIKI!!"*

And he must've thought for sure that I was crazy.

23

LA LUNA

LA LUNA

I'm at *Casa de Esperanza* now, the house where hope lives. *Y me llamo Luz*. My sister *Estrella*, The Star.

• • •

I figured I could keep waiting for Papi to get out since that's all I've done. And when I'm done writing the cards, I thought maybe I'd send them to Tencha. That way she can read them and finally accept what happened. Because though I'm Papi's daughter, I'm honest. That's what she taught me.

When I think of Estrella I remember how she'd act silly sometimes when she was in a good mood, wet from the pool plopped on the sidewalk, looking like a girl watching television with her head up at the stars. I'd be like her, in the same position, supported by my hands with my butt on the ground, looking up at You. She said behind the face of the Moon, You were there. But she was acting silly and serious at the same time. She wanted to tell me You were right there between us. I looked at her face and saw You, the way she saw You in the Moon. She'd look at me, waiting for me to say something, then start singing "Pena, penita, pena," and I could almost feel her heart come out of her skin. You and me and her, together in the way she looked at me.

It's like that sometimes. I see You in people's faces before they tell me something that means a lot to them. And that's why I loved her, because I saw You there, in the way she looked at me. Maybe when she was looking at me she was looking at You?

●　●　●

One time, Tencha said to me, "Come here, come here," like if I were some sort of dog. And I know love is expressed in strange ways, but still. Anyway, there I was, her little dog. She held me tight, and I couldn't breathe. She said, *"Te quiero, Luz. Lo sabes, ¿verdad?"*

"Yeah, I know," I said. And we looked up at the Moon.

54

LA RANA

LA RANA

And who comes last, *La Rana*, the one who reminds me of the sounds we heard from the window when we were trying to fall asleep.

• • •

When we were little, when we were kids, we liked to sleep in Buelita Fe's room whenever we got tired. We fell asleep with the television on in the living room while Papi and them were watching *Siempre en Domingo*. The wasps hit against the screen and the light outside turned lavender.

Buelita Fe had two beds. Hers was slanted because she had to keep her head above her feet, otherwise she'd snore and wake herself up. Luisa slept on that bed with me, and Gastón and Miriam slept on the other bed with Estrella.

We had never played the game before and I don't remember who mentioned it. I think it was Luisa. All I can remember was her on top of me pushing her hips into mine like in the movies. That's what it was, we were just acting like the adults in the movies. Her head tilted side-to-side like she was looking at puppies in a store window. Her tongue was out, and she kept asking, "Wanna make out?" "No," I said. "You're gross." "It's not gross if the actors do it," she said. Then she'd get off me and tell me it was my turn, see if I could do any better. I looked over to Estrella and Gastón, and they were just looking. Gastón was lying on his stomach. He turned away like if I were going to flash him or something. But then he would turn around and keep looking. "Don't act like you don't want to do it too," Luisa said. She opened her legs and squeezed me between her. And then I did it, because, so, we were just playing. We had our clothes on. But I was worried Papi was going to hear us from the living room and catch us. He was right there and the door was wide open. But the lights were out in the room, and we were in the dark.

I whispered, "Like that?" She said, "Yeah, like that. But do it harder like the men on TV." So I did. But then the bed creaked and Estrella started giggling and Luisa said, "Shhh!"

"¿Qué hacen?" Pancho said. He was still alive then.

All of a sudden it was like if some light had been turned on. And we stopped moving. That's when I noticed how bad Luisa's breath was.

I didn't want the bed to creak again so I just relaxed over her. I felt like I was flattening her. But she didn't tell me to get off, and we fell asleep that way.

• • •

Croooc, crooooc!

"What's that?" I whispered. Gastón heard me and said, "It's a toad, stupid." "No it's not. Toads live in ponds, stupid." "No, you're stupid." "It's a frog." "Then why did you ask?" "Because I was asking where it came from, not what it was." "Well, that's what you asked." "Shut up and go to sleep," I said. And he did, and so did Estrella, and Luisa, and me. We went asleep to the sounds outside, then waited for the sounds to wake us.

ACKNOWLEDGMENTS

My deepest gratitude to the Riggio Program at The New School, the Iowa Arts Fellowship at the Iowa Writers' Workshop, and the scholarship committee at the Bread Loaf Writers' Conference. Without your support and encouragement this book would not exist.

My love and thanks to:

All of my professors who have shaped and nurtured me: Andrew Sean Greer, Julie Orringer, Charles Baxter, Kevin Brockmeier, Marilynne Robinson, Zia Jaffrey, Sigrid Nuñez, Sharon Mesmer, Helena Maria Viramontes,

Josh Weil, and especially Lan Samanatha Chang and Rene Steinke, who worked specifically on this project.

My peers who read with such generous and thoughtful minds: Dina Nayeri, Stephen Narain, James Molloy, Carlos Queirós, Devika Rege, Chanda Grubbs, Greg Brown, Christa Fraser, Ashley Davidson, Jessica Dwelle, Scott Smith, and Luke Sirinides—thank you so much; I will always remember that workshop and carry it close.

My agent, Chris Parris-Lamb, who has been nothing less than a literary prince and hero throughout this entire process. Also, Andy Kifer, an incredible right-hand man and wonderful reader—thank you.

My editor, Claire Wachtel, who embraced this book, believed in it, and protected it in a way I could only have wished for—thank you.

Jarrod Taylor: this book would not exist without you.

My family and friends, near and far: you know who you are and you have my heart.

And to the absurd and audacious hope of wanting to become a writer—thank you.

About the author

About the book

Read on

Insights,
Interviews
& More . . .

Meet Mario Alberto Zambrano

Photograph by Nephi Nevin

MARIO ALBERTO ZAMBRANO was a contemporary ballet dancer for seventeen years, dancing in the Netherlands, Germany, Israel, Spain, and Japan before returning to school to pursue a career in writing. He received a BA from the New School, where he was a Riggio Honors Fellow, and completed his MFA at the Iowa Writers' Workship as an Iowa Arts Fellow. He is a recipient of the John C. Schupes Fellowship for Excellence in Fiction. *Lotería* is his first novel. ∾

www.marioalbertozambrano.com

A Q&A with Mario Alberto Zambrano

Los Angeles Review of Books
July 14, 2013

Daniel Olivas and Mario Alberto Zambrano talk about his celebrated first novel, Lotería.

DANIEL OLIVAS: *In your debut novel,* Lotería *(HarperCollins), we are introduced to eleven-year-old Luz María Castillo, who is in the custody of the state and alone in a room, with nothing more than her thoughts, a journal, and a deck of Lotería cards—each card printed with a colorful image used for what some call the Mexican version of bingo. You begin each chapter with an image of a card, used as a springboard into Luz's story. What inspired you to structure your novel in this way?*

MARIO ALBERTO ZAMBRANO: I grew up playing Lotería with my family, and like the Silvas in the book, we'd meet at my grandparents' house every Sunday, head to church, and spend the afternoon together. Lotería was a great game because everyone participated, even my grandmother, and there was a real sense of familial closeness as we played.

As a kid I wanted the cards to mean something more than their face value. I was drawn to the images in a way a child is curious about a book. Could these cards be used as tarot cards? I'd lay out the cards and try to foretell my future, but no one I asked knew anything about fortune-telling. So for a long time those fifty-four images remained mere pictograms of a childhood game.

Twenty years later I was living in Spain ▶

A Q&A with Mario Alberto Zambrano *(continued)*

and had just ended my career as a dancer. One night, I couldn't sleep and found myself circling a table I'd varnished with Lotería boards over the top. I stared at the images and searched for a narrative that linked them together. I didn't know what the story was, but the curiosity I had as a boy returned and it drew an outline. I was determined to connect these images in a sort of story, make a portrait out of them. That's how the idea began.

I tried many different approaches before I found Luz's story. I remember the morning when I went to a coffee shop on the Lower East Side, shuffled the deck, and flipped the top card over. It was La Araña, which became the first card of the book. I wrote that vignette, and when I reread it, Luz's voice seemed right to me. It felt alive. And from then on I just listened.

DO: *You grew up in Texas and, after graduating from the High School for Performing and Visual Arts in Houston as a presidential scholar, were a professional ballet dancer for seventeen years, which took you to such places as Spain, Israel, Japan, and Germany. Why did you ultimately decide to take such a completely different creative path?*

MAZ: My relationship with dance is pretty complicated. I wish I could give a clear explanation as to why I stopped or what prompted me to do something else, but emotionally it's still somewhat of a confusing loss for me. It was my first love, my first heartbreak.

I'd started dancing when I was eleven and had my first contract when I was seventeen. I danced for all the companies I'd ever wanted to dance for and worked with the choreographers I'd dreamed of working with. But it came so fast—and I really didn't expect it to actually happen—so that by the time I was twenty-five I was wrung dry, not just physically but emotionally. I started feeling a lack of passion for the work, though I still loved being on stage. I was becoming embittered with the idea of having to walk into a studio and be told what to do, spend all my energy trying to figure out what a choreographer wanted or what his vision was. So I quit, which sounds cut and dry, but my relationship with it was becoming sour and I didn't want to spoil it any more than it had already been spoiled. What I wasn't expecting—what hit me like a car wreck—was the crumbling loss of identity that I felt afterward.

For five years I was pretty blue about my future prospects. I thought I'd never find anything I'd be passionate about the way I was passionate about dancing. I choreographed, but I wasn't comfortable working in that way, having to depend on dancers to execute my work. Pen and paper don't get their feelings hurt if you ball them up and throw them away. But as a choreographer, if you cut a solo or a duet the dancers often take it personally. And you have to be sensitive to that. If you don't, you become stoic, which can turn you into a villain. The psychological drama of it all—as well as the politics—did not interest me. It interfered with the imaginative space that I feel needs to be protected in order to create. Some people can manage that kind of work with a kind of composure and grace, but I couldn't.

I went back to school. I studied humanities and literature through an online university called Open University. That's where I took my first fiction class, which at the time seemed like an absolutely bizarre thing to me: to write a story. For one, I was not a child who read and I never wrote. I was too busy doing dance moves in the garage. But when I took that fiction class I discovered an artistic practice that could satisfy my creative itch and that I could do alone, which suits my disposition. Now, the more I do it the more I fall in love with it.

DO: *Aside from earning a coveted starred review from* **Publishers Weekly,** *your novel also has glowing endorsements from such writers as Charles Baxter, Justin Torres, and Ru Freeman. How have these and other authors shaped you as an author, particularly during the early stages of writing this book?*

MAZ: It's funny, I actually didn't know about these authors when I started writing the book, which I'm embarrassed to admit, but it's because I wasn't immersed in the world of literature—not yet. When I started my relationship with fiction I was trying to catch up with as much contemporary fiction as I could, but of course, there's so much! There was an edition of *Granta* titled "Best American Authors" around the time I started writing, and I remember reading all of the stories in that edition so I could get an idea of the stylistic landscape of contemporary fiction. Jonathan Safran Foer, Karen Russell, Uzodinma Iweala were in there. That issue directed and introduced me to the kind of fiction I was interested in.

I'm often attracted to the way a book is designed—not only the musicality and tone of its voice, but its architecture. Books like *Extremely Loud and Incredibly Close* by Foer, or *If on a Winter's Night a Traveler* by Italo Calvino, or *The Waves* by Virginia Woolf; all of these have a sculptural existence in the reader's mind—or at least for me—and I'm fascinated by this. A novel's potential to exist as an imaginative ▶

A Q&A with Mario Alberto Zambrano
(continued)

sculpture or blueprint while still telling a story—this is one of the reasons I started writing in the first place. I had no idea it could happen, and when I saw it, and felt it, I was blessed by the beauty of what literature could do. ⌒

This interview first appeared in
The Los Angeles Review of Books
(www.lareviewofbooks.org).

"Matters in English"

A Short Story by Mario Alberto Zambrano

Author's Note

On one of my visits home to Houston, while I was in the middle of going through copy edits for *Lotería*, I was craving *caldo de res* from one of my favorite Mexican restaurants. I drove there in midafternoon, and the place was almost empty except for a mother and daughter sitting at a booth. I sat on the opposite side of the restaurant, ordered my soup, and pulled out my manuscript to go over edits. In the middle of going over every line in the book, I realized that the girl sitting opposite from me was similar to someone I had grown to love, someone I had tried to give voice to. The girl was around ten years old. She didn't speak much and wore an oversize sweatshirt with tight jeans. Her mother's hair was uncombed and there was a pack of Marlboro Reds next to her silverware. They didn't argue and there was nothing about them that necessarily suggested any sort of tension between them, but in that young girl's expression there was sadness and shyness. I watched them as they finished their food, got up, and went to pay at the register near the entrance. The young girl wanted a quarter for a gumdrop, and her mother gave her one. Then they left. It was a simple moment, but one that I needed. It was a blessing, in a sense, because the manuscript that was before me, the one I had written about silence and the need to share a story, was *for* that little girl. I mention this ▶

7

anecdote because in the midst of paying close attention to line and rhythm in the prose of *Lotería* while going over copyedits, I was also reminded of where the heart of this story came from.

In mentioning where things come from, long before I ever found my protagonist, Luz, or the idea of *Lotería*, I wrote the short story included below. I had just arrived in New York City to study at the New School, and I was thrilled when the story was accepted for publication in *12th Street*, a literary journal published by the Riggio Honors Program. In rereading it for the sake of the P.S. section of this book, I was surprised to find that here, for the first time, *Lotería* appeared in my fiction. And so I felt it appropriate to include it.

Matters in English

WHEN I WAS SEVEN YEARS OLD I would try to fall asleep between my older sister, Veronica, and my cousin Alondra as we looked up at the stars. We'd have a sleepover at Chucho's house, in August, which meant that a vacuous heat took place of a blanket we didn't need. As we tried to concentrate on keeping our eyes closed, Alondra would pinch my forearm with the tips of her fingernails and whisper into my ear, "Para qué sepas, no estás soñando."

A bevy of dust-colored pigeons and parakeets would coo at our feet in the coop Chucho had built behind his house. He called it his backyard even though it was all concrete and only a single tree was situated against the wall, half of it grown inside the coop and decorated with white splotches of bird poop. The birds would perch atop the branches and turn their heads at every sound they heard. Huelita, my grandmother, would tell us that they weren't just regular birds, and it wasn't just the noises they heard that they turned their heads to, but other presences we couldn't see. We would stand at the entrance and she'd nudge me toward them with her buxom belly, because they wouldn't harm me, she said, trying to convince me they were happy to see me. They were especially happy with children, she said. But I'd straighten my knees and brake.

"Pero están muy felices," she'd say, as she'd push me inside. I'd shuffle my feet and not look up in fear that one of them might crash into my face.

◆

Jessica's ear is pressed against my chest and she says my heart feels like a baby finch.

"When I held it at school, Papi, it throbbed, right here," she says, pointing with her index finger to the middle of her hand, looking at me with her eyelashes so far and long they pass the line of her eyebrows. She says she felt the bird's pulse in no other part but there, in the cup of her hand.

Kristen is staring out the passenger window. If I didn't know any better I'd think she was enjoying the wind on her face, since she looks so relaxed and at ease, but suddenly she turns inside the car and snaps at Jessica for no apparent reason. "Put your seat belt on! If you want to ride in front you have to act like a grown-up."

A few hours after we left Austin, Jessica wanted to sit between us because she said she was bored in the backseat. She had already played her games on the electronic device we bought her for Christmas and she wanted to know what we were talking about, even though we hadn't spoken much. I told her she could sit up front once we passed the border, and now that we're in Mexico she's standing on her knees, half-hugging me as I drive, her body melted into mine.

At every crossroad Kristen turns her head left and right. She thinks we should be careful about the strangers who approach the car, even if all they want to do is clean the windshield. "What's the big deal?" I ask. "They're just trying to make money."

"But we don't need the windshield cleaned," she says.

Jessica looks at me with her blue eyes, the ones she's inherited from Kristen's side of the family. "When I let go of the bird, Papi, he flew in circles around me, then above my head, because he didn't want me to let go."

Kristen pulls the seat belt around Jessica and forces her to sit down with her legs in front of her. It's a mechanical and motherly function, and when she's done she looks out toward the vast desert, slumped in the same position she was in before.

"Then what?" she says, the wind catching her words and throwing them past us. "Then what, Jessica?" She turns inside the car. "Tell Papi who called Mommy at work because someone wouldn't stop crying and couldn't concentrate on her schoolwork? Who had to pick you up?"

I wanted to drive down to the village because I knew we'd be in the car for more than eight hours. I thought a road trip would be good for us. But Kristen hasn't been herself, or as happy as I'd hoped. Maybe it's because my grandfather has passed away and we're on our way to his funeral. In some ways it's like she's holding something back, even though she tries to play the role of supportive mother and wife. In that way, she's more Mexican than she knows or would care to admit, concealing herself like that, so that really all she's doing is letting herself boil inside.

She turns toward the view where the sun is beginning to set, and ▶

Jessica watches her for a moment, then pulls my sleeve. Her hands are at her sides and she stretches her mouth in wide movements as if I were deaf and could read her lips: "It's not because he flew away," she mouths. "It's because he crashed into the window trying to come inside"—both of her hands open like undeniable stars—"and he died."

◆

There were times I'd be sitting on one of the stools inside the coop and Huelita would be next to me, throwing handfuls of birdseed in the air. She'd suck in her cheeks and pucker her lips, cup her hand behind her ear, and whisper, "Escucha."

She'd whistle a song. A melody from a black-and-white film. And when she'd stop, the parakeets would sing it back to her.

I'd try to whistle too, but no sound would come out of my mouth. I'd sit there and observe. Puckering my lips. Sucking in my cheeks. Blowing softly. But not a single note would come out. Nothing but air.

One morning when Huelita was whistling with the birds, I heard another whistle, sharp and quick like a whip. It felt as though a blade had sliced the air close to my ear. I turned and saw Chucho poking his head out of the kitchen window, whistling a different melody. He whistled it again when he saw that Huelita had ignored him. She threw up her hands.

"Hay Humberto!" she said, handing me the rest of the seeds. The birds flew manically into the coop, half of them whistling Chucho's melody, the other half whistling Huelita's—it all became a maddening song. She walked toward the kitchen with her hands chopping the air in front of her, cursing under her breath something about breakfast, and that it was on the stove, and that all he had to do was scoop it into a bowl.

◆

I received a phone call from my mother a week ago telling me that Chucho had committed suicide. He couldn't stand the solitude, she said. After Huelita had passed away two years before, he just didn't know what to do with himself.

I was in the car rushing to work, worried that I wouldn't have time to get a cup of coffee. I swerved from one lane to the next until I came to dead-on traffic, then I tried to tell myself what I already knew. That he was gone, and that now both of them would be missing whenever I went back to visit.

Since we entered Mexico Kristen hasn't said a word. Her right cheek rests in the palm of her hand as she slumps against the car door. A road sign says: *Apodaca: 20 kilometros.* She turns to me, even though it's self-explanatory. In the seven years we've been together she's never attempted to speak Spanish.

Jessica slaps my shoulder and points to the sign. "Papi, we're almost there! What are kilometros?"

I pull off the road and stop at a gas station with a pink sign over the awning. Jessica runs inside, to the sweet and spicy candy next to the cashier. There is no one in the store except for a man with a beer belly and a black braid down his back, standing behind the counter. Kristen walks to the bathroom in the back. The floors have recently been mopped and there's a smell that reminds me of Mexican streets during early hours, when mothers and wives are out sweeping the streets with water and soap, saying good morning to each other. It's a multipurpose kind of soap they use for clothes, cars, and house cleaning, the kind that foams up and makes a sidewalk look like a pathway of clouds. Whatever it's called, that's what they've used to clean the floors of the gas station, and it hits me that we're getting closer.

I buy Jessica some chocolate and vanilla Duvalin, a sort of pudding snack. She starts to walk on the balls of her feet until I hand it to her. Kristen comes out of the bathroom with her arms crossed and her hair tightly pulled back in a ponytail. I notice the man behind the counter look at her. I can't determine if it's because she looks beautiful or if it's because she's so fair, so un-Mexican.

As I pay, Kristen brushes past me, saying in a whisper, "There was dry shit all over the seat."

I turn to her so that I can give her one of those keep-your-voice-down looks, but she's already walking out the door.

In the car, between us again, Jessica is licking a small plastic spoon. Her smile is big enough for the three of us. I brush her bangs away from her face and ask her if she likes it.

"It's different," she says. "But it's okay."

When we arrive to Apodaca, it's nighttime. The streetlamps are lit with amber bulbs. The AC in the car is on and the windows are rolled up. Vendors selling tacos and beer are stationed along the sidewalks, staring at us in huddled groups. I want to stop and order a few of their tacos, but I notice Jessica sitting between us in a sort of daze with her mouth slightly open. She notices small children kicking a beach ball between parked cars. They're chewing the ends of thin red straws. I whisper, "We'll get you one tomorrow, *mija. Es tamarindo picoso.*"

My mother has insisted we stay with them in my grandparents' ▶

house, the same house where Chucho blew his brains out. She told me over the phone that his sister, Elsa, found him on the floor with a pool of blood beneath him and his arms open to his sides, as though he were swimming in his own death. Neighbors heard her screaming when she found him. They all rushed to the house and held her arms back so that she wouldn't tear down the walls, because when they found her, she was on her knees beating him.

I look to Kristen, but still, she's staring outside the car. She's as quiet as she was when I told her what happened to Chucho. We were getting ready for bed. She held my hand for a few minutes, then turned over and shut off the light. She'd only met him once, when he'd come to our wedding in Austin, Texas, and since then we haven't had a chance to visit, until now.

We drive past the plaza at the center of town, the cathedral, and then park in front of the marble sidewalk that borders my grandparents' house. When I was a kid the porch used to feel as big as a basketball court, but in truth it barely has room for three rocking chairs.

I take our luggage out of the trunk and hear my mother step out onto the tiled portico. She's wearing nothing but black, with a knitted shawl around her shoulders. My father stands behind her, like a shadow. As I get closer her fingers levitate and I catch her. I feel her chest quiver.

Next to the front door is a lanky woman who's been a friend of my grandparents for as long as I can remember. Her short, curly hair frames her solemn expression as she licks her lips and grabs our bags. I touch her shoulder, but she flinches and rushes inside. I don't think I've ever heard her say a word, not a gasp, not even a hint of weeping.

Once inside, I hear the pigeons and parakeets cooing in the back of the house. No one says anything, but I can feel them, or perhaps it's something in the shadows, whispering that they're happy we're here . . .

"Están muy felices, mijo."

◆

When I was growing up in the States my parents spoke to me in Spanish, but I never responded, though I understood. My aunts pinched me and my uncles called me names. They tried to make me speak in what they believed was my mother tongue.

Huelita never cared. She would sit by the window without saying a word, one hand crossed over the other. Light would lie across her face, and her image was so majestic to me. I didn't have to say anything. Somehow we understood each other.

Chucho called me names, threatened to whip me for reasons I never understood. During nights at the dinner table when the family played

Lotería, he'd humiliate me because it was always expected that everyone participate, make a joke, tell a story, say that a tabla *was cursed, or yell out* Lotería! *Anything. But I never said a word because everyone was always speaking in Spanish.*

"Juan! Qué haces?" he'd yell. And I always thought it was a stupid question—I was sitting right there with all of them! Hearing my name called out with such a brutish tone made me not say anything.

"Te voy a dar un chingaso, cabrón! Di algo!"

I never looked up because I knew he would be fuming in the face; his skin would be flushed with blood. He'd look like a monster, even though he was my grandfather. Sometimes I'd think of standing up and saying something to him in English. Like that, I would break him in more pieces than he could break me. Because who was the one who never learned English? But I always left my head down, and my parents wouldn't say anything. Eventually Huelita would call out another card from the Lotería deck and the game would continue.

◆

For breakfast my mother prepares *chorizo con huevos* with a side of refried beans. Kristen and I sit together with her at the kitchen table, and she asks us how we are doing. Kristen nods in a sort of consoling way that seems patronizing. "Don't worry about us," she tells my mother. I want to believe that she's trying to be accepting of everything, the house, this poor village, and all the Spanish around her. It's her first time visiting a small pueblo in Mexico, but still, nothing stops me from looking at her in a certain way.

Jessica is outside crashing her hands against the coop. Each time she hits the netting, the birds hardly react or notice her. She presses on the wire, losing patience, and calls out. "Papi! Why don't they do anything?"

I tell her to come inside and get ready for church. My mother stacks the dishes in the sink and begins washing them without saying a word. We keep our voices down as we walk to our designated bedrooms and get dressed.

Sunlight shoots through the trees, creating shadows of lace on the concrete in front of the wooden doors of the cathedral. Jessica is wearing a formal dress we bought her and I'm wearing a simple suit. Kristen is standing elegant in a dress she wore on one of our first dates. It's incredible to see her like that, her pale arms along her sides, her thin neck, standing out in a crowd of short men and women dressed in black. She's like a stem in a bouquet that hasn't been cut short enough, and it's impossible not to be proud that she's the mother of my baby girl. ▶

Inside the cathedral, relatives and friends crowd the pews. Locals stand in the back with their cowboy hats clutched over their stomachs. Their heads bowed. I wonder if they even know my grandfather, or if they're here because, like every Sunday, it's the hour of mass and they need to pay their respects no matter what, pray for those they love and those they feel need to be forgiven.

When I see Chucho in the coffin—so tranquil—I can't help but wonder if his spirit is lurking near us, or above us, checking to see if everyone he expects to be there is there.

Jessica fidgets in her seat and yawns in my face once the service begins. I yawn too, but I swallow and look as respectful as I can. My mother is beside me, clenching my hand each time the father says Amen. He gives a sermon about eternal love, and eternal light. How those we love continue to live after we die. Humans are incapable of seeing the transformation, but we must believe in the name of the Father, he says. One must have faith.

I look over to Kristen and her gaze is veered toward the stained-glass windows that make up half the walls. I wonder what she's thinking about behind that quiet somber indifference of hers.

In the parlor, where there are trays of small pastries filled with pineapple jam, Chucho lies in his coffin, receiving visitors. I have yet to go to him and say good-bye. I extend my hand to Jessica to see if she wants to join me, but she hides her face behind Kristen's arm.

"Don't make her go if she doesn't want to," Kristen says, and I can tell she doesn't want to join me either.

I should feel more emotional, I think, but when I approach my grandfather and see him beneath me, so pallid and ghostly, I can't think of one thing to help me shed a tear.

I leave, since it seems that any sort of cathartic undoing will never arrive. I look for Jessica because I want her in my arms, even though she's getting too big to be carried. But I don't see her or Kristen, and I start to worry. My mother tells me she saw them leave, so I go looking for them and leave the consolation duties to her. My father is hopeless at these sorts of things, which is why he decided to go back to the house after the service.

I find my father sitting at the kitchen table with a glass of brandy filled about a centimeter from the bottom. He hardly drinks, or at least I've hardly ever seen him drink. There's no one else in the house and I don't see Kristen's purse in the bedroom. He shakes his head and shrugs when I ask him if he's seen them, then, after feeling the quietude that pervades,

I decide to have a drink too. My father stares at the top of the wooden table as if he's reading the newspaper, even though there's nothing in front of him. It reminds me of when he used to come home from work, get two pieces of sausage and a few jalapeños from the fridge, and then sit at the kitchen counter with the *Austin Chronicle*. I always assumed he enjoyed reading the newspaper, because he was always so diligent about it, as if it were a chore, reading it from page to page every single day. As I got older it made sense to me that he was teaching himself English. In his own way, he was dealing with living in a country that wasn't his own.

"You okay?" I ask, sitting across from him as I pour a drink from the bottle on the table. I take a sip and the warmth burns my throat. He doesn't respond, but nods his head and curls his lip. I hear a bird flap its wings in the back, then nothing. The fading daylight turns the stone kitchen floor to a matte shade of metal.

We sit there, without talking, and after I ponder what to ask, I realize it's best to stay quiet.

The front door opens and I hear Jessica run down the hallway. She runs into the kitchen and comes straight toward me, gives me a strong hug. She's trembling. "What's wrong, *mija*?" I grab her face with both hands and look into her eyes. I can tell she's been crying because her cheeks are swollen.

"I love you, Papi," she says.

I see Kristen at the doorway, her head bent toward the drinks on the table. She doesn't say hello but stands there as if she's been waiting for an hour and it's time to go; it's me who hasn't noticed this whole time. I widen my eyes.

"Where were you?" I ask.

She takes a deep breath and tells me they went for a walk around town. They found a bench in the plaza and had a little talk.

"About what?"

She tries to smile, but it's like the ends of her lips are too heavy. Our eyes meet for a second before she turns and heads to the bedroom. And by how slowly she walks, the rhythm of her heels, I can sense she wants to be alone.

Jessica holds me; still, I can feel her chest trembling. I pick her up and take her outside to the back of the house, where the coop is, and I try to whistle. I suck in my cheeks and pucker my lips, blow as softly as I can, but no sound comes out. Jessica looks up and gives me a face as if I'm doing it all wrong. She fills her lungs and shapes her lips into the smallest bud, then whistles. I start kissing her cheeks where traces ▶

of tears have marked her face, because she's whistling! I've never heard her whistle before. I don't even know how she learned. But then we hear the birds. We hear the melody Jessica whistled go around us like a music box.

"Do it again, *mija*."

Jessica's eyes start to clear up. She pushes me away. She wants to get down. She runs to the coop and presses her hands against the net, something I never did growing up, and starts whistling. Looking at her, I see a tiny version of Huelita singing to the parakeets, and the songs fill the backyard with a kind of melancholy that only I can feel.

I turn toward the doorway because I feel someone, a presence. Something heavy sinks into my chest, like a paperweight. It's Kristen, staring at me, almost past me, and I know there's something she is trying to tell me. A faint voice in the back of my head says that she wants to leave. Not this place, but me. And it's not someone else. She's not having an affair. It's that she's fallen out of something, and she can't bring herself to say it. She looks at me with a sincerity in her eyes that begs me to figure it out so she doesn't have to say the words, the cruelty of them.

"I don't love you anymore . . ."

◆

There was one weekend during a summer in Apodaca when my mother wouldn't buy me a pair of black ninja sandals. Everyone was wearing them, and I felt I deserved them, especially since they were only a few pesos. But after buying me a milkshake, a journal, a wooden board game, and at least three different sweets, my mother figured there was no need to buy me anything else. But I wanted those sandals. I even tried stealing them, slipping them into my shorts when no one was looking. But the vendors were so sharp-eyed it was impossible. Furious, I wanted to show my mother how upset I was. It wasn't enough to say, "I hate you." If she turned away, it wasn't enough to walk in front of her and stamp my feet so she could see how swollen with rage I'd become.

That night I crept out of the bedroom where I stayed at Huelita's house. No one could hear me because everyone else slept on the other side of the hallway. I gently pushed the kitchen screen door open and walked on the balls of my feet with my back hunched, like a monkey, over to the coop. I grabbed the metal hook off the door and lifted it.

What I wanted was for the birds to fly away, but they hardly moved. They stayed, perched on their branches as if I were an idiot, staring at me, waiting for me to make a sound. I screamed without making a noise. My hands were clawed and the muscles around my face tensed up, trying to

16

scare them like a monster, but all they did was shift their weight and place their wings next to their bellies.

◆

In the middle of the night, I stare at the ceiling waiting for Kristen to move. She acts as though she's asleep and thinks that by being absolutely still she'll give the impression that she's dreaming, but I know how much her body moves.

My mother is in the backyard with the birds. She hasn't changed her clothes since the service and has been there since she came home from the reception, staring at the coop as if waiting for a message.

I give up trying to pretend that everything is all right and get out of bed. When I step outside I see my mother holding on to the wire fence, with her fingers curled like a chicken's talons. Her back, trembling. The coop door is open and when she sees me standing there she starts telling me that they won't leave. "It's time for them to get out of here, Juan. *Ándale, ayúdame.*"

She walks inside the coop and grabs the parakeets. They start to fly from one side of the coop to the other. I stand against the opposite wall, still with my phobia of getting too close to them. She throws the birds in the air, but they fall to the floor, and after they land on the concrete they walk around with their heads turning as if they're lost. Some of them find their way back inside the coop. She starts kicking them. "*Ayúdame, Juan!*" She grabs a broom propped against the wall and starts swinging it, then throws it down and grabs one of the branches of the tree. She shakes it and shakes it as though she's the force of an earthquake.

"*Váyanse!*" she screams.

I turn my head, thinking she's going to wake up the neighbors. She's going to wake up the entire village. I can see blood on her hands. I can feel the wings of the birds near my feet brush against my legs. There are so many of them.

Kristen comes to the doorway with Jessica, and there they stand, staring at my mother in awe. Jessica is wearing an oversize T-shirt and her hair is down. I go and reach for her, but I notice Kristen holding her hand. As I try to pick her up, Kristen glares at me as though she doesn't want me to touch her.

"What!" I scream. "What is it?"

My father comes out of his bedroom and turns on the hallway light. Kristen turns. When she does, I pick up Jessica. She buries her face under my chin as I begin to walk in circles. I whisper, telling myself to calm down, to breathe. "*Mija,* can you whistle for me?" ▶

"Matters in English" *(continued)*

She shakes her head. She doesn't want to.

"Please, *mija*. For Papi."

Holding her—my baby girl—I close my eyes and start to spin as if I'm waltzing, thinking that maybe this will change her mood. I imagine myself with wings and continue whispering into her ear, under the wailing cries of my mother, "It's okay, *mija*. It's okay. Tell them it's okay . . . *que están arriba*."

And then I hear her, my grandmother, like a memory caught under a glass jar, saying the words I'm saying to Jessica; as I continue to spin, I hear Jessica begin to whistle.

Then there's a rustling sound. I feel a wind circling above me as though we're caught in the middle of something spinning, and the sound of my mother's voice starts to soften. When I look up I see hundreds of wings like blowing leaves clapping in the night sky.

"Look, *mija*. Look up," I whisper, and I tell her she isn't dreaming. ❧

Previously appeared in 12th Street, Vol. II *by the Riggio Honors Program at The New School.*